THEY WHO HAVE GONE BEFORE

Footprints in the sands of time

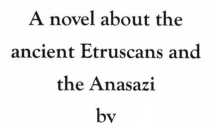

A novel about the
ancient Etruscans and
the Anasazi
by

JON FOYT

They Who Have Gone Before

Copyright © 2023 Jon Foyt

All rights are reserved

ISBN: 979-8-3911366-1-3

Published by

Big Hat Press
Lafayette, California
www.bighatpress.com

DEDICATION

To they who have gone before,
leaving their footprints in the sands of time.

And to the archaeologists who study them.

Recently near an ocean beach in France, a dozen surprisingly-preserved footprints were discovered. Using state-of-the-art techniques, archaeologists were able to date them back to Neanderthal teen-agers.

Imagine a record of a beach stroll being imprinted and preserved for eons in ocean sands.

Or, suppose the strollers left similar evidence in the white sands of America's Southwest...?

Ancient footprints have been uncovered in New Mexico's White Sands Monument that can be traced to inhabitants there many thousands of years ago.

CHAPTER ONE

A Year Ago

New Horizons, Please

As he usually did in the shank of every afternoon after returning home from his class sessions on campus, Dr. Jackson Alioto grumbled into his scotch neat. "Wish I…" he began, only to be stopped by his wife Danica, who interrupted, "Not again, Jackson!" She put her arms around him. He was wearing that western deerskin jacket and always loved the imagined feel of its authenticity on her finger tips. She smiled at her husband and said softly, "You and I have got to find a new horizon. I've said it over and over and I'm going to say it again…right this minute!"

Another chortle from Jackson, who was sometimes called by his students "Stonewall."

"J. A.," she began, thinking she would lead into this overdue conversation of theirs rather than listen to more of his laments of discontent one more time.

As if to right a wrong, he said almost apologetically, "I do love interacting with the students but there are always the same old questions that I've been exploring since—well, in academic hindsight, it seems as if it's been since the beginning of archaeological time."

She waited, hoping for him to reach down into his real self and express his true feelings, which slowly he began to tip-toe toward,

"Well, we all agree that students are our hope for the future, and I relish their youthful enthusiasm…but I wish their enthusiasm could be transmitted to me. It's always the same old, same old, that brings me back to another stack of papers I am professionally-bound to grade. Their papers are on subjects I've lectured about for years." He hesitated and then went on, "I guess I've come to…well, I hate to say it, but you know it all seems to be multiple layers of carbon copies, if I may make an archaeological analogy," He chuckled at his clever comparison.

Danica smiled, both in agreement and in sympathy. "But what about our months-long program of selecting certain students and inviting them to our house for Sunday night dinner and discussion?"

"Went well."

"And?"

"Good for the students and fun for us, but…." He extended his whining, "You know, Danica…I wish there were new horizons in new lands that I could personally gear up to explore and become enthusiastic about…re-live those exhilarating emotions of my younger life…fill my days with anticipation…do it once again…at this advanced stage in my life…in our lives, I mean."

"I know," Danica began, then paused. He waited, and she waited.

He smiled at her and asked, "What is your solution?" he pressed, "You do have a solution…." It was a statement…waiting for a confirming answer…or so he dearly hoped!

Danica's pause continued as she reminded herself of how much she had yearned to travel to a new place, alone or with her husband, to a brilliant place, over some sort of rainbow…perhaps…where exciting emotions lived beyond the realm of expected emotions.

Sensing his wife was about to offer something that would mitigate his mood, Jackson waited.

She said, "Listen to me and no stonewalling!"

2

He smiled. "You're on."

"Today in our faculty lounge, I met with an old friend of ours from school—"

"—Not another disgruntled archaeologist weary, as I am, of the same old academic roadblocks and hoops to go through?" Jackson interrupted. His voice resigned, he added, "Toe the prescribed academic line…don't rock the old boat…it might just tip over and we'll all drown in a king tide of monstrous old ideas and, I lament, chewed-over knowledge." He waited, "So, dear Danica, do tell, do deliver, do excite our class of we two, hopeful to-once again be eager students."

She smiled at her husband's familiar, yet regrettable mood, and went on with her news, "You remember Kip Overman, my PhD. professor from our school days here at U of Arizona."

"Yes, of course…and?"

"He was in the lounge making farewell rounds of professors before heading to the student lounge to see students whom he remembered, so he could tell them, too, as he did me right there, that he was literally and figuratively moving on in his career."

Jackson puffed, "Nice work, if you can get it."

Danica added, "Actually, Kip wants to reveal his new situation to you and me. He has invited us to visit him over in Portal."

"You mean to film one of those beautifully-colored trogon birds during winter mating before it flies back south into the deep forests of Mexico?"

"You can bring your camera if you want to, but that rare bird is not the purpose of his invitation. As soon as he and I could talk privately, he shared his exciting plans. He's transferring to the Max Planck Institute—specifically, to their campus in Berlin…"

Jackson's eyes opened wide and his voice grew eager, "Go on."

"He's joining their new program called "Academic Outreach." It's designed to explore exactly what you and I may be looking for—new horizons in archaeology."

Jackson clapped his hands in approval. "That is exciting news! Good for his career. But when will he inform us in person as to the details of his involvement?"

Quickly Danica replied excitedly, "Tonight, at his house."

"Excellent!"

"I'll whip up some hors d'oeuvres."

Jackson perked up, "I'll drive us to Portal."

Danica exclaimed, "That's my man!"

"Oh, by the way, is he still married to…ah…Dorothy?"

"Yes, the same way you are still married to me." As her fingers explored his deerskin jacket, she kissed his stubbled cheeks.

* * *

The Pueblo-style Adobe Home

Jackson steered their Honda Civic to a stop in front of Kip and Dorothy Overman's house. A For Sale sign was stuck in front of a white lilac bush. The nearby mailbox bore the names of Dr. Kip and Dorothy Overman. Behind stood an inviting flat-roofed Pueblo- style home, likely made out of adobe bricks, its stucco cover the traditional dark brown tint of Southwest high desert homes.

Portal was a scattered-about place rather than a typical tight-knit town. The few similar houses here and there, were foreign in arrangement to the traditional Roman-origin laid-out checkerboard street pattern. Down the gravel road leading to the Kips' entry lane not far away was a rural fire department station, in similar Pueblo style, a sign of security from late summer wildfires known to wreak havoc on such out-of-the-way residential areas.

"I see the realtor's sign. So, you're actually selling?" Jackson remarked as Kip and Dorothy greeted their visitors.

Kip announced, "Yes, we are going to Berlin to explore a fresh concept that we'll share with you this evening. Thanks for coming. Danica told me you two, like us, are searching for new digs." Laughing at his unintended play on the word "digs", Kip was joined in by Danica and Jackson as Dorothy brought a tray with four glasses of, she announced, "New Mexico Chardonnay for our beloved fellow archaeologists."

Kip had built a fire that now illuminated the large beehive shaped corner kiva fireplace, the focal point of the living room. On the mantle above was a display of Native American pottery. The pungent aroma of burning pinon pine logs added to the mood of anticipation electrifying the room.

In her eagerness to know more, Danica wasted no time, "So, tell us, why are you two leaving Arizona?"

Kip smiled as Dorothy offered an accompanying nod.

Jackson echoed his wife's excitement, "Yes, please. I'm anxious for you to elucidate on this opportunity of yours. You see, alas, I'm reconciled with those of us in this academic field being stuck in our particular discipline. We're much like those ancient Altamira cave paintings in Spain…painted there eons ago, always to be looked up at with murmured, 'ohs and ahs.' But though they are beautiful, they remain the same old paintings on the same ancient cave ceilings." Jackson sipped his wine and addressed his hosts, "Dorothy and Kip, you might say, I'm looking for new ceilings and new art work."

Dorothy agreed, and turning serious, began to explain, "I guess it's my doing. You see, Kip was getting discouraged—I mean, like you suggest, Jackson, there are only so many sites in your chosen field to excavate, write reports about, and publish findings in professional journals, before you begin to see redundancy creeping in. You want to explore new interests, look at fresh horizons in your life. At least, from early on that's what has Inspired Kip and me. It is exactly what the two of us were beginning to feel about the future of our lives. And then, to no one's surprise, one day a few months ago we actually began to express these thoughts, thinking back on all those routine stifling faculty meetings we are obliged to attend."

Kip smiled and elaborated, "Our two grown children have their own careers and their own family lives. Hans lives in another part of the country and, alas, our sweet Ursula is overseas. Obviously, neither is close by. So, apart from our house in Portal, there's not much keeping us here. We've each built up retirement benefits from our careers at the university, yet we don't want to just sit around, counting the days, and then wonder what we're going to do next with ourselves. There are too many exciting things going on in the world that we want to investigate. We want to be part of exciting developing fields of archaeology."

Dorothy and Danica went to the kitchen to put their snacks on a serving plate. While there, Danica asked, "Tell me, Dorothy, a question: don't you regret not keeping your own family name on your archaeological reports?"

Dorothy looked surprised at the question, but Danica said, 'I do, and I'd like to do it all over again...become my own professional woman."

As they returned to the living room, Danica added, "Freedom to live my own life, and not be linked...ah...elsewhere, I guess."

Dorothy nodded, "Yes, I do sort of...and I sort of can agree with you...now...but I didn't back then."

In the living room, Jackson was asking Kip, "Danica tells me you're accepting positions at one of the Max Planck campuses in Germany. I've read that after the war, the Germans named the bulk of their scientific research after Planck-in honor of his earlier research into theoretical physics."

Kip said, "Yes, Planck is a country-wide institution these days."

Jackson asked, "So, what specifically will you be doing at the Berlin campus?"

Kip answered, "There's an innovative department whose mission is to explore ancient cultures that have been overlooked—to make a list, back up new findings with evidence and arguments for focusing on each. And then to organize archaeological explorations by either incoming students or those already on staff, or a combination thereof."

"Do you have one such project already determined?" Danica asked.

Kip nodded. "Yes, a map of the ancient Etruscan roads versus today's Italian highway system—"

Jackson interrupted to ask, "Did your papers about the Classic Mimbres people of New Mexico have something to do with Max Planck's interest?"

Kip smiled and said, "Apparently it did. To refresh your memories, you two may recall the story of the Mimbres pottery that showed the famous—"

Danica interrupted, "Wasn't it around the year 1092? You know, the explosion on the moon—bright red, supposedly caused by a meteor hitting our moon and bursting into flame?"

Kip nodded, "Yes, it was back in the 1920's or maybe the'30s when an early archaeologist found that black and white bowl depicting the moon with a red blotch fired into it. The archaeologist was confused because all the Mimbres pots he'd seen so far in exploring the area were black and white. One of his associates whom he told about the find was from China. His associate said he was just reading some early writings from a Chinese monk in which he told of a meteor hitting the moon in around the year 1092. So, here we had a Mimbres potter from a thousand years ago who must have been watching the moon that particular night and, to mark his experience and record his surprise, he craft and fired a pot showing the bright red meteor explosion as the outer space object struck the surface of our Moon. Incredible, I say, and so say a lot of archaeologists."

Dorothy added, "The director at Max Planck in Berlin referenced this event. He said it was an example of what this department we're joining would be championing: discovered stories triggering increase interest in popular subjects, not only archaeology, but also about earlier peoples of our planet—a challenging interest, especially for those cultures that few students and even academics know much about." She continued, "The effort will add to our understanding of those who have gone before and their apparent discoveries about life around them." Dorothy then suggested, "Kip, can you give our guests the Institute's plan for exploring one of these cultures?"

Jackson and Danica seconded Dorothy's request, followed by Kip expounding on the state of archaeological funding. "To find the money for explorations, it helps if you're going to add to the body of knowledge already popular in academic circles. In other words, those grant requests are more easily satisfied, leaving proposals to explore new locations and new ideas overlooked." He placed another log on the fire, and said, "It seems we'll be making contact with some of the Institute's brightest students—those on the cutting edge of exciting horizons."

Danica applauded.

Kip went on, "So, looking forward, the Planck folks in Berlin are planning a conference in year or so at an Italian museum to which they will be inviting world-wide archeological professionals to give papers proposing special academic investigations."

Dorothy chimed in, "Kip and I have been specifically invited to rely on our Mimbres experiences in exploring the general broad topic of the pre-Roman Etruscans."

Kip added, "Moreover, they have asked us to line up the professional talents of two other archaeologists who will explore in depth one or more Etruscan sites. That is, after they have surveyed the Etruscan world across Italy. Then they'll be ready to discuss their findings, at the proposed convention site, which is to be held in the Etruscan Museum in the ancient Etruscan town of Tarquinia. That's where you two come in, should you choose to do so."

Dorothy said, "This means that should you accept the mission and join us, you'll have ample time ahead to put together your own view of the Etruscan culture, which you will find is extensive and, more importantly, mostly overlooked by the halls and publications of academia."

Jackson reacted with a "Wow!" and Danica clapped her hands. "Just what we are looking for, right, Jackson?"

"It certainly is!" Jackson responded, pondering the possibilities during his next sip of wine, "Yet it all sounds too easy, thanks to you two, of course." After a moment, he asked, "So, what is our next step—that is for Danica and me?"

Handing a large brown envelope to Jackson, Kip replied, "Here is the paperwork...all of it quite manageable. Please read these pages before you each sign and send them off to Berlin. You'll note extensive health coverage is being offered, good compensation, and all that kind of stuff. Oh, and plane tickets can be arranged by calling their special number—it's in the package. Call us if you have any questions. Meanwhile, with your approvals, of course, we'll submit your names and academic credentials via email to Berlin, telling them you are seriously considering the assignment. You can follow-up and confirm your desire to join in."

Danica exclaimed enthusiastically, "You know, I feel like a freshman on her first day of class, bright horizons ahead, to be sure. I'm so excited!"

Kip gave a thumbs up and said, "They've shared with us their plans to invite several archaeologists from the States, including a professor from the University of New Mexico who is rumored to have made a breakthrough find out at Chaco Canyon...just rumored, that is, or so I understand."

"That'll be the Anasazi," Jackson offered.

Danica corrected her husband with, "They are known today as the Ancestral Puebloans."

"Oh, of course." Jackson smiled broadly, looking at Kip and Dorothy. Getting up to leave "to drive back to Tucson," he followed with, "Thanks so much to you two for thinking of us. This is the big and welcoming change we've been looking for in our lives."

Danica agreed, adding "A challenge, for sure, and an opportunity for each of us to learn as we explore and discover an exciting field... yes, and for us to grow with our explorations," She concluded with enthusiasm by downing her wine and smacking her lips with gusto.

There were hugs all around.

CHAPTER TWO

Some Months Later

Moving Forward

Interrupting her meticulous taping and labeling of moving boxes, Danica called out from her computer, "J. A., here's an email just in from Kip and Dorothy. They've arrived in Italy and want us to know about their first exciting social engagement:"

Jackson put his arm around Danica, squeezing her gently. They read together:

Dorothy and I were welcomed to this Tuscan town of Viareggio by Dr. Arturo Pistoli of Siena University. Viareggio is traditional home since 1830 of the annual Carnivale, which parades around the harbor of this coastal town. Arturo and I were in the graduate program at Columbia. He is an archaeologist of much note and has an overview of the Etruscan civilization, which I will summarize for you today before Dorothy and I head off to Berlin.

Arturo introduced us to the town's famous Carnivale, which had been postponed from the previous year by the pandemic shutdown. In this seaside town, in my observation as an anthropologist, the people have rallied around the unique creativity of their Carnevale that expresses the gamut of original thought—from politics to art. Their collective efforts show how a society working together can build happiness as well as advance the national ethos toward greater heights…*literally*. It was much as Arturo had characterized the nature of the Etruscans all those years ago in his Ph.D. thesis.

"This centuries-old tradition has continued to update itself to the immediacy of world events." As we watched one warm evening, we marveled at two dozen five-story-tall floats paraded past us on a route around the waterfront. Hundreds of people, residents and tourists alike, paid 15 euros to watch while hundreds more danced enthusiastically ahead of their respective color-coordinated floats. Actors on top danced and sang, accentuating each float's message.

Messages ranged from Save the Amazon, "I Can't Breathe," a black man chained to the Statue of Liberty, to Angela Merkel hoisting a tankard of ale while presiding over the European Union, all the while lederhosen-wearing dancers celebrated as the heads of other European nations peered out from their barrels of brew, foaming glasses grasped in their toasting hands.

Meanwhile, famed Italian female astrophysicist, Margherita Hack, loomed over a bevy of male scientists left in her career wake, an overt up-to-date tribute to the modern-day scientist Jennifer Doudna of Berkeley, the subject scientist of The Code Breaker, by Walter Isaacson.

Many smaller, yet equally impressive floats, were interspersed between the building-tall and precisely built edifices, some being pushed along the parade route by hand, or else propelled by foot power, their float size too small to qualify to be pulled by a tractor.

Finally, making the last lap of the Carnivale course, came the lead float with its smiling image and its label of "Graze, Mario." The message was a clear thank you to Mario Draghi, the former director of the European Central Bank, who has just become the Prime Minister of Italy.

Perhaps Mario's ascension to power represents the starting gun for Italy to join the first string of European players after decades of fascism followed by a dysfunctional monarchy, the world-wide destructive war, post-war bouts with hovering threats of terrorist attacks, experiments with communism, socialism, and the publicity of a former flamboyant macho leader.

Always present, for Italians as well as tourists, will be the half-millennium-ago Medieval Art Scene, its names, its creativity, as sculpted into time as the ultimate, so far, of human expression, under the umbrella of the Medici and the Vatican, it was preceded by the Romans who, in time, followed our Etruscans.

They who have gone before have left their canvasses, their marble, their art, and the Roman and the Etruscan culture for all of us to see, to study, and to learn from, today and tomorrow. But tomorrow is here today, and while the sun's rays strike Mt. Vesuvius with the same fury, Italy moves forward in a newly-oriented popular Carnevale.

By the way, Danica, you are the leading candidate to kick-off the conference when the venue and logistics have been decided. Rumor is you will be followed by this academic from New Mexico, Dr. Stuart Sweet, who, so it is rumored, has a rather exciting find on the Anasazi. But whenever anyone from the press tries to reach him, his office says he is on sabbatical and not available for comment. Anyway, he is said to be about to retire and so he will have time to speak at the conference, assuming he returns from sabbatical.

We'll send an update in a few days. Best from Kip and Dorothy.

* * *

One Week Later – All Hallows Eve

Danica called out to Jackson, "Here's that update we've been waiting for from Kip and Dorothy in Italy. It's a Halloween message." He read the computer screen over her shoulder:

On our last evening in Italy, in the company of Dr. Pistoli and his *family, at dinner sitting on their deck high in the Apennine Mountains, we viewed west over the Ligurian Sea and south over the Tyrrhenian Sea.*

Beneath us appeared a vast landscape featuring the top of the Leaning Tower of Pisa, the offshore island of Elba, where Napoleon was exiled and where the ancient Etruscans mined their iron ore for Mediterranean trade routes, and the town of Viareggio. Going south, the old Etruscan Road (now the route of the main north-south Italian autostrada) connected the major towns of the 13-member Etruscan League. Farther south, the road links to today's Rome.

Stretching out before us were the ubiquitous hills of Italy. Atop probably most of those hills were the remains of an ancient Etruscan settlement, each community bordering on the old Etruscan Road. At each of these settlements, carved into its hillside, are their tombs, the venues where the Etruscan afterlife played out. Most of the tombs are still there, buried one after the other, mysterious, haunting, promising to reveal the life story of a then newly-deceased occupant.

Today in these hilltop towns, we can see the heritage of what was a vital Etruscan custom on the Day of the Dead, both in Mexico and in many other Mediterranean cultures. That is, honoring and even trying to communicate with those who have gone before us.

Kip then began to piece together a message from Dr. Pistoli. Actually, it turned out to be a brief summary of Etruscan advice prepared for, as he put it, "Our curious American friends." He told them, "It's coming *to you, in Dr. Pistoli's words,* "from our Etruscan friends of American students. From across the centuries, from us to you. Here are some things you need to know about we Etruscans:

"First – We are a group of folks who love life and are comfortable that life leads to death which for us is a continuance of life. We paint this belief into the art in our tombs and on our sarcophagi. Death to us is just one continued step in life itself.

"Second – We value each other. Our women and our men are equal

in social status—equal in importance. As such, marriage is an egalitarian arrangement between two evenly-matched people. Each partner exchanges a ring to honor the other. Simply look at the paintings in our tombs and on the walls of our meeting places, showing the dancing, the happiness. Look in the eyes of our men and women…see the motivation expressed in the contentment of their lives. See the natural pigments in the colors of their paintings. Marvel at the dedication of their love for each other as shown by their expressions on the carved images on our many sarcophagi.

"Third – We pursue commerce on the ships we build. Our trading friends are all across the Mediterranean, including the Greeks, the Carthaginians, and even the Iberians.

"Fourth – We can fight if we need to. Etruscan warriors are fierce fighters because they love our land and our people who live in the towns nearby or make up our 13-member Etruscan League.

"Fifth – We don't choose a pharaoh or a dictator or elect a chief from among us because we govern ourselves with respect for each other. You won't find people-built hills with a chief's house on top because we all live in natural settings without the burden of designating rank or prestige. So, do not link us to the Egyptians of old just because we honor death and the mores that live with death.

"Sixth – We speak our own language, not some vague derivative from one of today's more popular Indo-European tongues.

"Seventh – You may discover more about us as you pursue your investigations of our many sites dating back some 2500 years, more or less. If you do, then go for it!"

"That's it?" Jackson asked.

Danica replied, "That's a lot of thought and pertinent information from Dr. Pistoli. It will certainly help us as we search on our own across the Etruscan territory of Italy under the auspices of and guidance of the Max Planck Institute."

"It'll be our focused guidance, that's for sure, as our learning curve escalates," Jackson confirmed with enthusiasm.

Kip concluded his email with, "We'll see you following the conference. Meanwhile, enjoy meeting the other attendees and, especially, enjoy your Etruscan explorations."

CHAPTER THREE

Later

The Tarquinia Conference

At first take, it promised to be another of those stuffy sparsely-attended academic conferences. Only this one was international in scope. Moreover, it was being sponsored by the prestigious Max Planck Institute. For enhanced prestige, many members of the media, both popular and academic, had been invited with invitations going out to archaeologists around the world. They showed colorful photographs of Etruscan art and the venue in which the conference was to take place. It was not some five-star resort hotel with swimming pools and tennis courts, plus restaurants with raved-about cuisine. No, it was, instead (surprise!) within a cave, and not just some wet, drippy, dank dark cave but the ultra-modern Etruscan Museum in the center of the ancient Etruscan city known as Tarquinia.

The museum cave featured a natural rock roof and blandly cold stone walls. The muted effect instructed arriving participants to focus on its displayed museum contents, which they would readily find was a collection of artifacts from the ancient world of the Etruscan culture. As a result, entering participants would find themselves with nothing to do but think, act, and feel as if they were back sometime around 500 B.C., or even earlier, living and breathing within an unfamiliar-to-most Etruscan environment.

Earlier, most of the museum's glass display cases had been rolled aside and were temporarily being stored in the rear of the cave. In their place, rows of padded folding chairs had been set up for the registered academic participants and those members of the press who were anticipating a possible news-making event, albeit in an out of the way venue in a remote part of present-day Italy. Moreover, the unique venue was a significant distance in kilometers from the modern-day airports of Rome, Pisa, and Naples. Getting to Tarquinia and the museum required taking a train from Rome Termini to Viareggio, with connection in the Pisa Centrale station.

Asked about air travel to Italy today, one blogger commented that with Air Italia having flown into aviation history books, the Italians might do well naming its new-found replacement "Air Etruscan" in honor of their national heritage That would be a better choice, the commentator said, than "Air Medici" or, heaven forbid, "Mafia Air." That received many comments—not all favorable—for his travel article.

Whichever airline or train the many participants chose to book, those who were presenters, should they look around, which a good speaker will do, they would see their reflections in the few remaining glass display cases. Their museum-cave venue would be so very different from the more typical—and familiar—classroom setting, placing conference attendees smack dab in one of the homes of the Etruscans—smack dab back in time, Etruscan Standard Time, give or take a millennium.

* * *

The Conference Keynote Speaker

Jackson smiled at his wife and said, "Congratulations on kicking off such a prestigious conference."

"It is a surprise. Maybe it's the topic of the paper I've prepared: "An American Professor Talks About <u>Her</u> Findings on Etruscan Women.""

"And you're to be followed by this teacher from...New Mexico...."

"Yes, but first by you, J, A. You know, I've read one of Dr. Stuart Sweet's papers," Danica advised.

"What's Sweet's subject?"

"Well, unless he speaks about this purported new find of his, it will be 'Roads'," she replied, adding, "Dr. Sweet has written about the network of roads leading to and from Pueblo Bonita, the large Ancestral Puebloan site in Chaco Canyon in New Mexico. He explains that you couldn't see the roads from the ground."

"These are the peoples called the Anasazi, right? Well, then how does one see these roads?"

Danica replied, "Aerial photography. He writes that in the 1930s Charles Lindberg pioneered this new technique--its first use, so Stuart states, in the field of archaeology. When the photos were developed, to their surprise both students and professors right away saw the roads—the ancient Anasazi highways from two thousand years ago. The roads led in and out of Chaco Canyon...all across northern New Mexico."

Jackson puzzled, "But those people didn't have the wheel—did they?"

"That's right, and that's the big Anasazi conundrum—people with a nexus of roads but lacking the wheel. No horses either. Nor big dogs or beasts of burden. And, moreover, no carts or chariots. All those new technologies came centuries later brought to North America, of course, by invading European colonizers."

Reflecting, Jackson said, "Well, Sweet clearly must conclude that those many miles of roads were simply for walking...but why expend all that effort to build roads? Why not just simply follow old foot trails beaten down by your ancestors over the years? That is, if you just want to walk."

Danica clapped her hands and then enthusiastically commented, "But, don't you see, Jackson, these dilemmas of the Anasazi—road and no wheels—and what Stuart Sweet is telling us and what we're uncovering about the Etruscans all fit into our assignment from Planck, and that is for you and me and Sweet to compare Etruscan and, later in time, Roman Roads. After all, one of our assignments here is to map the Etruscan roads, the later overlapping Roman roads and then, for tourist interest, to overlay the modern Italian highways and the network of back country roads."

Jackson added, "Yes, Roads! That all fits in for each of us and for Dr. Sweet, as well our one immediate nuts and bolts assignment, so I understand, for us archaeologists and the Italian government, along with Max Planck is to be working on a combined tourist-archaeological publication about roads, past and present in Italy."

Danica added, "Maybe there's more to find out about both the Etruscans and the Anasazi." She paused. "Anyway, meanwhile we'll receive token royalties, as authors, one Euro, isn't it, from every museum map sale?" She thought for a bit before suggesting, "This conference is going to prove rather challenging for us, J. A."

"You mean, stacking up the Etruscans versus the Anasazi—"

"—Ancestral Puebloans…."

"Okay, if you insist."

"I do."

Summing things ups, Jackson said, "Well then, these two different peoples—living oh so many miles and so many centuries—at least a millennium—apart, may have been thinking along the same lines, right?"

Danica smiled in anticipation. "You and I will be looking into this phenomenon in great depth."

CHAPTER FOUR

Stuart Sweet Flies In

Although he had been on sabbatical for almost a year, Stuart got a phone call nudge about the conference from the head of his department. The Dean advised, "Here's an experience that'll look good on your retirement credentials—put you right up there with other world-class professors, I should think."

Immediately Stuart contacted the Max Planck Institute expressing interest in attending and hopefully contributing an overview talk on his insightful personal experiences among the Anasazi. He speculated if it might have been his rather noteworthy, or perhaps somewhat controversial reputation around campus and among contemporaries that triggered their interest in his appearance. In short order, he received an invitation to attend and, as well, to speak on the conference's opening day about his specialty, the Ancestral Puebloans, known earlier as the Anasazi.

The conference location at the Tarquinia Museum turned out to be a surprise for Stuart Sweet. In error, he had jumped to the conclusion that the location would be at the two-thousand-year-old Roman port of Ostia Antica, which, as he learned from his quick research, was near the site of the 5th Century B.C. Etruscan town of Veii. However, the Max Planck Institute had chosen a different venue.

He was pleased to learn that Dr. Danica Alioto, following hers and her husband's research in Italy on the Etruscans, was speaking. He had known of her from reading several of her recently published academic papers dealing with the language groups of ancient Italy, a subject in which he had curiosity commensurate with the many different groups of the Anasazi peoples.

The change in the conference venue had come at almost the last minute, so it seemed to Stuart, for he had gone so far as to make hotel reservations near what he had thought would be the conference venue—Ostia Antica. Stuart laughed about the matter and changed his flight reservations to fly into Pisa and train south from there. The announced conference venue, together with its conference title, exciting to many in the field, was "The Discipline of What the Ancients Have Taught us—Papers Introducing New Thought."

* * *

He found out that Dr. Danica Alioto, coming from her new assignment at the Max Planck Institute in Berlin, would be speaking in English. She was billed as being from the University of Arizona and scheduled to deliver her initial paper entitled "What We'd Each Like to Know about Every Etruscan Woman and Couple, and especially what they thought of themselves, and what most academics today proffer to be their progeny, the emerging Romans."

Following Dr. Alioto's talk and introducing her husband, Jackson, with the ensuing discussion, Stuart was billed for one of the day's following talks. "That's me," he declared proudly as he realized the organizers had accepted his topic outline entitled, "My life with the Anasazi in Chaco Canyon around 1000 A.D." (He was sure most attendees would recognize his location as including the architectural wonder in, as the Spanish would say, northwest *Nuevo Mexico*)."

The breadth of the conference had been clearly spelled out—his talk and Dr. Alioto's talk, on ever-so-different topics, were destined to ignite new ideas and serve to define new frontiers, intending to adhere to the organizers mission to explore new fields and launch new ideas in archaeology while broadening the landscape and profession of archaeology.

Stuart told himself that his visualizations of his experiences of being with the Ancestral Puebloans, exciting as well as scary—as he would narrate them to the conference attendees—would spark their interest and their desires to learn more about the Anasazi. The attendees would be, he hoped, inspired to research more and try to fill in the blanks about their culture. By telling his stories, his vivid imaginations that had come to him on the sites of various digs, he would ignite new trains of thought, new explorations, birth new horizons for the academic search for truth about his favorite peoples— the Ancestral Puebloans of Chaco Canyon.

He was happy that one of his students, Victor, was arranging to come with him. They would each be returning for the later scheduled follow-up meeting with his seven other students at his newly-purchased retirement home on the California Big Sur coastline, there to decide—actually vote—as to whether they would publicize their groundbreaking Chaco Canyon finding,

CHAPTER FIVE

The Conference

Accommodations for attendees were limited in Tarquinia to typical Italian tourist bed and breakfasts, all of which were fully booked, a small hotel, also booked, plus more B and Bs and other tourist accommodations in nearby towns. Campgrounds were also full, as well. The organizers appeared satisfied that, as things got underway, everybody, especially the important media members, had been taken care of. All were now in attendance, curious as to what fresh revelations about ancient societies would be disclosed for academia and the popular press, television, and professional magazines.

* * *

The chair of the conference, Dr. Hildegard Rumsfeld, her blue and yellow striped blouse accented by her bright pink nametag, rose to the microphone to call the conference to order. After the room had quieted, she introduced Dr. Danica Alioto as an American archaeologist on leave from her tenured post in the university of Arizona in Tucson, and now with the Max Planck Institute. Dr. Hildegard told everyone that her current mission was in line with Planck's objective to proffer and develop new ideas and new thoughts about the evolving field of archaeology. She reminded everyone that the Etruscans represented the perfect example of another widely known yet still-to-be thoroughly researched culture "waiting in the wings." She continued, "They preceded the much-written about Romans and their vast Empire. As everyone today acknowledges, the Romans easily outshone the earlier Etruscans. Yet in archaeological time, the Etruscans actually paved the way for Rome's eventual dominance of the Mediterranean area, as well as the history books and the written archaeological record…To hear more, please join me in welcoming Dr. Danica Alioto…."

CHAPTER SIX

Getting Their Attention

Following polite applause, to grab the audience's attention, Danica abruptly asked, "How many of you here at this conference are either married or have been?" She held up her left hand and pointed to her years-old wedding ring as a symbol of her own marital state.

A cluster of hands went up, some promptly, some hesitantly.

Danica instructed, "Look at your third finger on you left hand."

Those who were married or once had been displayed their wedding ring.

She thanked the audience and continued: "Marriage, and I am referring here to the concept of an egalitarian marriage has been brought to you by those who have gone before—our dear and most affectionate—our lifetime role models—our ancient pre-Roman Etruscans. And this may surprise you, but here I am referring to the peoples you see on display in this cave in this most unusual of modern museums."

Gasps of disbelief came from many.

She paused, waiting for the audience's full attention. "One of the many customs of the Etruscan is the idea of true affectionate marriage. It was theirs. And so—perhaps--they taught the custom of sincere and equal marriages to the many cultures who, in later years, tried to follow their example. I mean, I implore you to look closely at the many Etruscan sculptures we admire." She flashed on the big screen a number of photographs of Etruscan sarcophagi with couples lying together on top of each. Then she showed divans with newly married couples embracing on their wedding night, rings on their fingers displayed.

She added, "These photos, my husband Jackson and I have collected during is our recent explorations of Etruscan sites from Rome north as far as Venice. We are working on a map of the Etruscan roads as overlaid by later Roman roads. Next, we will be going for more detail –namely compiling data and art works from as many tombs as we can visit."

At this point Danica paused to introduced her husband, Dr. Jackson Alioto. Amidst a scattering of obligatory applause, Jackson thanked his wife as he assumed the podium. He began to summarize their joint findings about the Etruscan peoples during their past months of surveying across Italy. He said, "First, before I return the mike to Danica, I want to briefly share with you some of our work-in-progress findings in addition to what Danica has told you so far. It may shock you…."

Members of the media began to listen more carefully and take notes assiduously.

Jackson continued, "In their day—that is, the first BC millennium--there were hundreds of Etruscan cities and small towns dotted on hillsides and in valleys across central and northern Italy, plus the island of Sardinia. Among those towns, 13 cities were members of the Etruscan League." Jackson paused to let this information sink in. Then he injected, "Let that number 13 remain in your mind. It's significant in the history of Western Civilization—a central point expounded upon in Danica's and my paper." He projected a map on the screen showing the many Etruscan towns and cities covering today's Italy. After a brief moment in which there was intimate buzz circulating from the audience, Jackson took advantage of the impact of his words to pose the question, "And what do you think was the purpose and the motivation on the part of the Etruscans to form this 13-member League of independent cities? I mean, don't you think it took a lot of diplomacy and persuasion on the part of these different cities and their leaders to come together and form this confederacy of purpose?" He paused and added, "I certainly do and I award kudos to the Etruscans for their achievement of so many years ago. In the face of rising Roman strength and both their military and cultural influence."

Without saying a word, one participant toward the back of the cavernous auditorium immediately stood. Raising his hand high, he waited as some took notice expecting him to be called upon or loudly speak out with either a question or a challenge directed at the speaker.

Ignoring the young man and continuing, Jackson composed a reply to his own question, "Obviously, the Etruscans were addressing a growing need to fend off invasions of the shielded and spear-equipped Roman warriors. Without warning, these Romans had been ranging forth on raids north out of the city of Rome—you know of course that town located on the Tiber River." Several laughed. Jackson went on, "I have begun to ferret out the real purpose of this Etruscan League, based upon our research over our many months of exploring around Italy. So far, we've been focusing on the routes of old Etruscan roads. But first, I will give you a hint of our rather revolutionary findings—"

—Coming from the back row of chairs, came the loud voice of a younger male, likely a student, or so he was thought to be by most of the conference participants. From atop a chair, he was waving his hands to get audience attention. Having done so, he bellowed in a determined voice, rudely disrupting the speaker, "Dr. Alioto, Sir, you are plagiarizing the findings from my research! You have stolen them from right off the draft of my report which I shared with you and your wife, Dr. Danica, only a few days ago. Your paper doesn't give mention to me or allow me due (and required) credit. You are ignoring my career. I remind you that you are professionally bound to give recognition to me in your findings…after all, they're my ideas based upon my discoveries!"

Jackson was dumb founded. Never in his teaching career had he been so blatantly interrupted, so insulted, so yelled at. He instructed himself to "Stonewall it." Looking about for Danica but not seeing her, he quickly formulated his rejoinder. Without making eye contact with the student to address him personally, he shouted back across the audience, "I believe you are the student who claimed to me that you and your family are descended from Etruscan ancestors from centuries back in…what was your absurd claim? Wasn't it 700 B.C?"

"It is all true!" the booming younger voice shouted. "I am Bernard Monterrosa. The Etruscan League includes cities of my ancestors…it's as true as anything today in archaeology." By now, heads were turning in all directions, surveying the audience seeking the disrupter, the person rattling conference etiquette.

Moving farther forward in the museum cave toward the podium, the young man continued his tirade as he shouted, "You're depriving me of the rightful recognition of my findings, my expertly documented hypothesis."

Jackson attempted, "No, no!" Then he addressed the dissident directly, "Bernard, the Institute has an academic board to hear your complaint. It's not up to me or to Dr. Danica to resolve your issues."

The student hastened to add, again in his loud and firm voice, "But your wife told me I had raised a number of valid points for the Max Planck Institute to consider." Bernard reminded Jackson along with everyone else, "Remember, Sir, you and the Institute have expressed a desire to open up new lines of thought and exploration about the Etruscans."

The uproar had quieted a bit, as those in the audience sensed there was more to this outburst than just the complaint the young man had raised. Perhaps there was another layer of dirt waiting to be excavated? or so some might say in the jargon of archaeology.

Jackson was stumped as to how to move on from this unexpected interruption. A few moments passed. Feeling intense embarrassment, he looked down at his notes and told everyone that it was time for him return the microphone to his wife.

However, everyone watched as the young man, with determined steps, moved closer to the speaker's platform. Many recognized him as the man whose voice had called out. Yes, they all nodded as if in unison, it was Bernard. He was a large fellow, over six feet tall, bearded with curly brown hair that when he brushed back from his face, revealed a determined glare aimed at Jackson.

Jackson sensed he had to retreat but he couldn't move out of the way as Bernard approached. More in the audience rose, some moving forward toward the speaker, sensing a brawl in the making and intent on coming to Dr. Alioto's physical defense. At the least, they reasoned, they could restrain the accused by calming him, dissuading him from any act of violence. Others sat still, waiting, perhaps recalling their class in role-playing that taught How to Calm a Disruptive Student, a course required of both faculty and students in today's more confrontational world.

Sensing trouble, two uniformed museum guards, nodding their assent to one another, moved closer to Jackson. They succeeded in blocking access, securing him from the person yelling out and others now coming toward the stage. In addition, two suited employees, a man and a woman, each with identification badges hanging from their decorated Etruscan sport jackets, were moving toward the microphone ready to address the crowd to try to restore the museum cave to the normal quiet discipline prevalent in the culture of academia.

Distracted by the commotion, however, few in the audience observed Danica slipping through the crowd and approaching Bernard. Those few who did saw her escort him, some thought rather tenderly, toward the dimly-lit rear of the interior. The two moved in side-by-side unison into this darker area, she seeming to speak quietly to him while gesturing the direction he should move in order to reach safety where he could listen to her instructions. He seemed attentive to her, yet gesturing back at what many sensed might be labeled as "the fates of academia."

A small group of curious and concerned conferees now gathered around Jackson. Perhaps they wanted to show support for the speaker or perhaps they simply wanted more information about the dissident student Bernard. Indeed, the issue raised about the Etruscan League and its purpose was one of considerable interest. And as the group shuffled about in quiet conversation, a young woman, her T-shirt showing Thomas Jefferson's Monticello mansion, pushed forward, her nametag showing Ross, she shouted out, "Hey, did you guys ever hear of America's Thirteen Colonies?"

A professor stepped up to address her, "Ms. Ross, Is there some sort of connection that exists between two of you?"

Many nodded. Ms. Ross added, "Yes, that's what my cohort Bernard is suggesting. Let's hear him out. Wow! Flag this, if you will!"

CHAPTER SEVEN

Bernard Monterossa

Bernard, in the faint light at the back of the cave, stands tall above Danica. Looking down into her eyes, the handsome student tells her in an impassioned hushed voice, "You and your husband have failed to hear me out! There is an historical connection that I have come to know about—"

"—Tell me, Bernard…" Danica, stepping closer to him to inspire confidence. "Do let me in on your secret."

It is whispering time in the dark recesses of the museum cave. Bernard takes a deep breath before relating his discovery to Danica. Listening intently, she is frozen in his gaze, or perhaps by her sheer admiration for a student, this student who would so confidently convey to her, a tenured teacher…or rather is she experiencing in a state of academic disbelief? Standing there, her eyes on his, Danica struggles to dispel her confusion.

"You see, Dr. Alioto…."

"—Call me 'Danica,'" she whispers then quietly reminds herself of her age and professional standing.

But with intimacy Bernard replies, "With pleasure…. Now, Danica, I must tell you what few others know to be my personal lineage with our ancient Etruscan friends. This information is absolutely revolutionary!"

Danica yearns to support him, but knows he has to reveal more if anyone is to believe her or, more importantly, him. She presses, "And you know all this…how?"

Bernard smiles as if he is about to reveal what he has seen, as if he had been invited to unroll Gods' structural plans for decreeing the creation of His Universe. Lowering his whisper even further, his voice barely audible, he lays out the story. "You see, you must come with me back into the mid 1700's…"

"I will travel with you, Bernard, so please go on."

"It happened this way: An ocean-going merchant trader named Montague Willing of the trading firm Willing and Morris, having slipped through the English naval blockade around Philadelphia, sailed his ship across the Atlantic and into the small harbor of the Italian Ligurian Sea port of Viareggio. There, Montague dropped anchor and patiently waited, as protocol decreed, for the Harbor Master to come aboard and arrange for him to dock portside."

In her academic voice, Danica presses her charge, "And how can you possibly know about this…?"

Bernard holds up his index finger and waits a moment, all the while relishing the look in her brown eyes. Slowly he feeds her the story, her mouth opening wider awaiting each morsel of information.

"The Viareggio Harbor Master was one of my ancestors. As he told my father's great grandfather, he was a descendant from a prominent Etruscan family."

"And your father told this news to you?"

Bernard nods and continues, "Yes. Please bear with me as I tell you. This ocean-going merchant named Willing was the sort of explorer who had always been imbued with runaway curiosity. Once ashore, he traveled inland into what, before Italy was united, had been the independent republic of Tuscany. Centuries earlier, the area had been home to a big slice of prehistorian Etruscan territory. Tuscany was the center of the Etruscan culture. Hearing about these peoples in their homeland, his natural curiosity was aroused. "Not only was Willing intent on exploring, he was also hoping to find quantities of desirable finery to load onto his ship to take back and sell in Philadelphia.

"And what did this fellow Willing learn?"

Bernard smiles and waits, his silence adding to the weight of his eventual reply, "He found out about the ancient Etruscan League with its 13 cities. He thought about all these different cities for a while. Slowly and thoughtfully, he began to compare them to the 13 Colonies back home that were then being formed in a league of sorts on the shores of the New World." Bernard pauses for effect, "You see, that is where the 13 Colonies got their idea for the 13-member Continental Congress—from the Etruscan League."

Danica's whistle ricochets off the walls of the museum conference cave, bouncing back and forth from wall to wall, causing crowd noise to diminish as people look around for the whistling sound's source.

Bernard leans over and tries to hug Danica. She doesn't resist, permitting him to whisper into her ear with his explanation, "That's how our part of the New World got its name...our own 13 colonies organized to protect against the rule of King George and Colonial England, in the same way the Etruscans had organized their cities in defense against the intruding Roman warriors.

Whistling once again, Danica proclaims, "Yours is indeed a wild story, Bernard." She ponders his words and then queries, "What proof do you have...yes, is there any proof...substantiation? You'll have to admit that your story is way out there." She adds, "Nobody's going to believe it, let alone anyone in academia...it's just too...well. Just too plain wild."

"Proof?" He pauses, adding, "Yes, I do have proof, Danica."

"You know, it's just wild enough to have merit, and I think I want to believe you, but...well, what is this so-called proof you have?"

"An Apulian krater."

Right away Danica wants to know as she asks, "This krater, a ceramic work of art from the town on the Adriatic shore? But where is this krater, and what does it portray?"

Bernard replies, "The Carabinieri Police have recovered it...from salvage they scooped up in the old harbor of Brindisi. So, Danica, if you and your husband will endorse my findings...well...that would add the necessary credibility for my paper to be accepted in scholarly circles." He adds in a rather pleading voice, "And we'd all benefit... you and your husband with the Planck Institute and me in my doctoral program...why not, dear Danica, please?"

She wants to run her fingers through Bernard's flowing hair, but she resists...reluctantly. As she debates her emotions, her urges, she asks herself if this is what being over the rainbow is like? Is this what new opportunities are like? Have she and Jackson come all the way to Italy for this?

But then Danica suddenly switches to the reality of her situation. She tries to reason with herself, promptly distancing herself from Bernard's advances. She exclaims, "No, no, no, Bernard! It just doesn't work this way... no, no!" By now they have moved farther back in the cave. She says, "There's no way to verify this ship captain's trip, his findings, there's no written record, no verification, no documentation."

Bernard whispers, his voice as dim as the lighting. "But now that I've told you about the evidence, I can add that I can give you even further proof that you want."

Danica's voice is louder and firm, yet pleading, "Can you really?" she resists again reaching for Bernard, saying, "You see, if I am to believe you..."

Bernard tries to embrace Danica, reaching out to pull her closer, but she eases herself away, yet hearing him assure her emphatically, "But I can!"

Danica stands there close to Bernard saying nothing, thinking, wanting to believe this daring and courageous young knight of the new archaeological world standing before her in the dim light of an ancient Etruscan cave.

Danica searches her will power, her mind, her profession. What if she really, deep down, wants Bernard to be right. What if she really wants him to prove his hypothesis with his Apulian krater and even more evidence? What if she really wants him to ignite the world of archeology with his wild, remote, yet possible story?

Danica presses, "Bernie, what is on this krater, this ancient pot of the Etruscans?"

"Letters, Etruscan letters," he says in reply. "They had an alphabet," as you already know"

"Yes, I've seen it. An alphabet...of sorts..."

Bernard adds, "The letters of my Etruscan family's name."

"Oh, come on now. That's a stretch. Don't you think?"

"A and W, translated into the Phoenician, comes out to my family name of Monterossa."

"What will happen when I tell all this to Jackson?"

"Maybe he'll have to defend it, along with the two of us...plus...."

"Plus?" she presses.

"Danica, I have the ship's manifest, Willing's merchant ship out of Philadelphia."

"Where? Where is it, Bernard?"

"The Carabiniere have it. I have entrusted them with all my evidence. They have a secure lock box they're holding for me. It's all there."

CHAPTER EIGHT

Dr. Stuart Sweet

The Ancestral Puebloans of New Mexico, aka "The Anasazi."

Following a two-hour break, Dr. Rumsfeld reconvened the conference for the afternoon session. The featured speaker was Stuart Sweet.

Awaiting his introduction, nervously anticipating his time at the podium, Sweet reflected on his life's work as a single, never-married academic professor. He had been born into a family of educators In Santa Fe where he pursued his primary and secondary school education. He nurtured a sense of pride, as well as affection, especially for his father and eventually for his mother and wanted to mirror their dedication to education. So, it was no surprise when he pursued a teaching career following his Ph.D. studies in archaeology at Kansas State University.

It was said by fellow academics that, as a professor, Dr. Sweet nurtured curiosity in his students by encouraging each of them to pursue a guiding goal, "Seek out the truth among the ancients," justifying this clarion call with the explanation, he would say, "From them, learning their traits, their culture, their civilization, their rock art, we stand to learn more about ourselves."

Over time, Dr. Sweet had developed among his academic peers the unflattering reputation of being rather a maverick among his academic peers, for he was continually prodding both students and faculty for their opinions, indeed, their answers, realizing that many times there were no answers to his multitude of questions, only unsubstantiated opinions. But it was those opinions—verified or not, wild or clever—that he wanted to hear expressed. They went beyond brain-storming ideas to comments off the wall, maybe even flippant remarks. Through it all, Stuart was seeking well-thought-out responses from others in the field, hopefully fortified with evidence and research of their own processes or that of other authorities.

Professor Sweet was thought to be a fair, yet demanding professor whose mission in life was to encourage the best from his students by means of intellectual stimulation. Consequently, his classes became over-enrolled and his special seminar courses were full months in advance.

Still, he had not risen in the ranks of academia to become chair of his department for he was thought to be a bit apart from the main stream, a good instructor, a popular teacher, but not a follow-the-leader university team member. In other words, doubts remained hidden under the surface of his academic colleagues. That was okay with Stuart for he loved his work even if his mental horizon went beyond that of his cohorts. However, he had not published much in academic literature, as was required of every academic, although he had in mind—and often worked on drafts—a scholarly book about the Anasazi of the American Southwest.

During his career, in order to fill the seemingly endless hours of loneliness when he wasn't teaching or excavating an ancient ruin, he would often relive one of the many exploratory digs highlighting his career. Over time he had come to fill the days and campfire nights with his academic devotion to exploring the mysteries of the vast and remote Chaco Canyon in Northwest New Mexico.

His mind traveling across the centuries, Dr. Stuart Sweet had stood, as he did now at the podium, full of excitement resonating in magical harmony with the peoples of the ancient Anasazi. To anyone who would listen, he would readily acknowledge that the Anasazi had a great culture they had created in the wilderness of North America during the arduous years since their ancestors had walked across the Bering Land Bridge from their ancestral homes in Siberia.

There was the time, Sweet so vividly recalled, the frightening yet stimulating night he had found himself, not watching, but participating with the ancient peoples in their lives. It had been a rare Chaco Canyon evening when the billowing fog engulfed him in a mystical mood of magic.

Word of Sweet's many such unusual experiences had spread throughout numerous academic circles, and he had been interviewed by a student reporter for the college newspaper about his supposed time travels. (She had described them as "downright weird.") It was that interview that he had reproduced as a handout for the Tarquinia conference participants for their overnight reading. It was to be followed by discussion after the question session for both his and Danica's introductory talk.

Today, looking at the faces of his audience trying to judge the degree of their curiosity, Stuart decided to relate an experience he had had one particular night. Taking deep breath, Sturt began his presentation, "In a thick enveloping mist, I was transported back in time to a quite strange and exciting place. I found myself in a far-distant environment. It seemed I had become a participant in that scene. I was a player in a familiar though different location from that of my habitual research and teaching environment. Instead, I had become a player—a living sentient being thrust among throngs of real-life ancient Anasazi.

"Inconspicuous to them, at least during the initial moments, I moved among a growing assembly of Ancestral Puebloans, dressed in their native attire, augmented by their darker skin. My blue eyes and white complexion stood out like a political placard in a parade and quite obviously revealed me as not being one of them. I had no painted face markings, as they each did, no hat, as some wore—presumably the more important ones. Each prehistory person seemed a unique and distinct personality. I began to fear for my well-being.

"Little children, many naked, were running about. Some were chasing dogs, some petting them. All the while, most of the dogs, appearing friendly, were wagging their tails. The adult Anasazi wore jewelry, fashioned either from strung acorns, or from strings of concha shells, brought in trading agreements with beach communities--how many miles away? Likely there was some sort of trade arrangement, perhaps for local corn, beans, and squash. But who were the traders and where did they venture, and how were they treated once there? Obviously, they walked for they had no horses or wagons, nor wheels on carts pulled by dogs, unlike some peoples elsewhere. And why not? If theirs did, why not here? I quickly realized I had spent a good many of my academic years asking such questions. And suddenly here I was amidst the answers—if only I could decipher them!

"The adults' singing was melodious, reflecting, I felt, a contentment with their prehistory lives, their environment, their culture. Every so often, the singing fell into a chant, with most of the children responding in unison as led by the adults.

"Uh, oh, I stiffened. Here comes the shaman—yes, it must be the shaman judging from his elaborate headgear together with his display of commanding jewelry. He was walking with authority in his gait and presence, and he was heading directly toward me! In desperation, I hastily recalled lectures to students about the importance of the shaman in prehistory life, his power, his male influence, his strengths. Accordingly, I stood in fear, though I didn't know what exactly to fear. Was it the Unknown coming at me from out of a fog of more than 1,000 years? This unknown was approaching from a distinctly different culture that I felt I knew something about. But reluctantly, I realized I didn't really know anything—clearly not how to act, what to say, what to believe, or what to hope for when I was side by side with one of them, as I was now. Still, I had taught students, conversed with them, answered their many questions, thrived in their curiosity and critique of my own explanations about these prehistory people and the role of their shamans.

"Despite my palpable apprehensions, I stood steady, frozen in place, as the shaman, tall slender, fiercely radiating authority, approached. His eyes captured mine, revealing to him, I was sure, my personal fright, perspiring as I was, in apprehension—a vulnerable academic alone in an ancient world of time.

"Adding to my fears, I saw two muscular men behind him coming toward me, in stride with the shaman. Were they henchmen, warriors, enforcers? What might they do to me? In those ancient days, and in this long-ago culture, there was not likely a process for appealing one's fate, that is, seeking safety through some sort of codified law. I saw my life was in their hands, absent any court of appeal, soldier or sailor who would ride to my rescue like the calvary in a western movie. I wondered if the Ancient People knew or even felt the concept of mercy.

"It was then it struck me—there were no subtitles on this visual screen of life displaying what the shaman was saying to me. Moreover, there was no handy Anasazi-to-English dictionary I could consult. I could not speak their language, nor they mine. There was no basic root like Latin, no Indo-European rules to summon up, no matter how some utterings may have begun to sound familiar but soon faded into the unknown. From my studies and readings, I knew a lot about the various Anasazi language groups, that is, their derivatives, their names, but of course I was not able to converse in any of them. So, I could not plead, reason, implore the Anasazi by expressing my academic logic. Worse, I could not reassure them by reciting my academic creed and explaining my good will toward them. I was speechless. Quickly I realized I also would not know what they were saying. The language barrier was deep and unwelcome. I did not know what to do. I could not run—where to? That is, if my legs would carry me, somewhere else offering safety from the Shaman and his two henchmen.

"As much as I had urged my students to get inside the minds of the ancients, I realized how impossible such a task was with either ancients or contemporaries. Observing the shaman, I had no idea of what the man was thinking, planning, or deciding to do. Nor did I know what to do to escape his fate at the hands of these ancient people. I almost laughed at the fleeting thought of jumping into my Studebaker Conestoga station wagon, flooring the accelerator and escaping the prehistory village by following one of the ancient roads leading out of Chaco Canyon. But then I remembered that I had forgotten the ignition key. And, of course, my Studebaker was not here with me in this village of ancient prehistory folks."

Stuart waited for the buzz from the audience to subside, only to be interrupted by a voice to Stuart's side. He introduced one of his students, Victor Adrena, who had volunteered to join Stuart by coming to Italy to participate in the conference.

Victor was almost at the podium when a voice from an attendee called out, "But Dr. Sweet, how did you get out of your predicament with the Anasazi shaman—please tell us, yes, please don't leave us wondering."

The professor smiled and said, "Glad you asked. Here's how I would have liked my predicament, as you called it, to have been resolved: I smiled at the Anasazi holy man, to have the experience unfold: I smiled at the Anasazi holy man, and the shaman smiled back. Together, we gestured upward and slowly began to climb the nearby hill from where we looked out over the Anasazi settlement. We stood there, side by side, for an indeterminate amount of time as he and I observed the dancing and singing below. Then, as the fog floated upward into the night sky, the scene began to fade away and I was left alone, wondering, speculating, re-imagining the strange experience."

The audience was briefly silent before the buzzing and head shaking began. Then Victor stepped up to the podium again and began speaking extemporaneously "I'm going to tell you about an experience Dr. Sweet related to a group of his students: In Chaco Canyon, it was midnight with a full moon and we students were sitting on a hill overlooking the Grand Kiva, Dr. Sweet was describing to us what had likely taken place a millennium or more ago in that Grand kiva. As best I can, I'll repeat his narrative:

"On a small hill above the Grand Kiva, we watched certain women beat with their hands on the deerskin covered former post holes turned into drums in the four corners that once supported poles that once attached the thatched roof atop the kiva. The tune they played was weird as costumed dancers entered the kiva following in step with the shaman who was wearing a huge headdress. The rest of the antiquity ceremony was displayed across the arena below. The dancing, the music, the festivities, the singing, the captivating display became ever more powerful as the ceremony continued its ancient increasing alure."

Here Victor stopped. Thanking his student, Dr. Sweet resumed the narrative, "But then, as the shaman seemed to be conducting some sort of spiritual exercise, with the dancers and singers joining in. I had a sudden realization that as many excavations as I have conducted, as many field notes as I have transcribed, as many years as I have spent trying to investigate the minds of the ancient prehistory peoples—whom I have come to love as my students—I was no closer to my goals I had set for myself those many years ago when I embarked upon my career in archaeology devoted to understanding the ancient Anasazi. That is, except for those rare out of mind journeys into the ancients' territory centuries ago.

With a wave to the audience, Stuart concluded, "And that is my presentation for the afternoon." He hesitated and then added, "I would like to tell you about our new discovery, except my students and I are still endeavoring to verify the authenticity of this important find. If it is verified, we'll be releasing the data in a year or so.

"Why such a long period of time?" a voice demanded to know.

Stuart replied, "It's a find from Northwest New Mexico that will upend the teachings about the Anasazi—they are the Ancestral Puebloans of Chaco Canyon and the American Southwest. As professionals, we have to get it right, you know, before we publish our paper. Otherwise...."

* * *

His mind crossing through ever so many centuries, Stuart stood at the podium, his excited emotions resonating in magical harmony with the peoples of the ancient Anasazi. He would readily acknowledge their cultural progress in the exciting new civilization they had forged out of the wilderness of western North America, down through all the arduous years since their ancestors had left their ancestral homes in Siberia and walked across the Bering Land Bridge to settle in an unexplored continent.

But his time was up, and the moderator, now taking over the podium, was dismissing the attendees until the morrow. Yet many lingered, approaching Stuart with questions and comments.

CHAPTER NINE

*Several Days Later as the Conference Continued
and More Papers Were Presented,
Dr. Jackson Alioto Left to Explore Etruscan Tombs*

Dr. Jackson Alioto with his team from the Max Planck Institute were scheduled to begin their exploration of Etruscan tombs set into a hillside below the hill town of Orvieto., some distance away. In Etruscan times, Orvieto had been a leading spiritual member of the 13-city Etruscan League.

Danica joined her husband, arriving in a van with others, as Bernard, along with many other students, traveled in their separate van.

This dark day brought sheets of rain slowing their progress along the Italian back roads.

Each person was dressed in appropriate rain gear, including boots with battery-operated lights affixed to the front of their hard hats. They also had waterproof cases with pens and audio devices for inscribing both written and oral notes, and, of course, digital cameras to visually record their findings.

The many tombs were not numbered, but by reading from right to left, the researchers could discern the names of the families, albeit written in Etruscan script across the stone lentil over the opening. There were no entrance doors to any of the tombs, only an opening that had been exposed down through the intervening centuries to years of rain today, plus snow and wind, as well as the footprints and marks of untold visitors—tourists, looters, and locals. In fact, there were no visitor logs recording who over time had set foot down into the tombs.

Inside the tomb, in typical Etruscan pattern, the explorers expected to find several rooms, one at least with walls decorated with colorful art work, though faded over time. There would likely be a sarcophagus with a sculpted image of the deceased lying on top, or perhaps there would be two figures, likely the husband and wife simulating their lifelong repose and affection for each other.

As the van carrying Dr. Alioto arrived at the line of tombs, a flash of lightening crackled overhead and a loud roar of thunder shook the area. Undaunted by weather, Dr. Alioto leapt from the van, head lamp illuminated, ready and eager to explore this line of underground tombs, one after the other.

To launch his new assignment—the Etruscan phase of tomb exploration, Jackson, notebook in hand, exclaimed in delight, echoing a tenet of Etruscan lifestyle values, "Onward toward the continuance of life!"

"Here! Here!" blended with calls of "Avanti" as groups set out to explore tombs in the seemingly endless hillside with its gaping openings leading to even more and more tombs.

On his own, Jackson began popping into first one and then a second tomb, recording with his camera the scene, his voice noting on his recorder details of the paintings and the sarcophagi that he viewed down there in the darkness, now lit from his head lamp as he eagerly peered, one after the other, into each of the tombs.

Danica could hear Jackson's voice recording his observations, "Each tomb is a study in itself, each having a subsurface entrance to which rough stone slabs have been set into the dirt. There is no door, simply the ancient opening suggesting a place of continuing life reconstituted as death. There are no interior lights, as these were not tourist-like museum tombs outfitted with illumination. There were no railings to grab onto, fastened there to steady oneself in the dark of the entrance. These are dated tombs from more than two thousand years ago." He said into his recorder as he eagerly pounced from one stone step onto the next one, intently focusing his gaze into the darkened tomb, its interior dimly lit only by his headlamp as the beam danced around in tandem with his own visual gaze.

In the drumming rain, some later said they had thought they heard Bernard's voice calling out, "Over here, Dr. Alioto, this one's a winner, an Etruscan gem."

Jackson promptly went to that opening—the one in the direction from where he must have thought he had heard Bernard's voice calling out to him.

Once there, he leaned forward, enabling him to peer downward and into the wet darkness. Jockeying for a better position, his boot slipped on the wet entry stone placed every so many centuries ago at the tomb opening. He lowered his head and moved to enter the dark nothingness. Momentarily Jackson lost his balance and seemed to propel himself head first into the darkness where death itself ruled.

* * *

Was there another human figure near the entrance? Some said no, a few said they thought there might have been someone else, but no one could say the name of the person. only heard were calls for help from the others nearby.

All came running. Lights shown into the tomb. Several quickly descended, only to find Jackson's head, bloodied by now, engaged directly into a sarcophagi and his body limp at its foot, his equipment strewn, his voice silent except for what some said they heard was an agonizing moan.

CHAPTER TEN

What Happened?

"An accident?" Danica posed, "Yes, most surely, he fell," Danica told the uniformed Commanding Officer of the Orvieto Tomb Guards, the immediate Italian authority with jurisdiction over the incident and who had promptly arrived at the scene. His arrival was soon followed by an ambulance from the hospital in Orvieto, its medics jumping out with their medical kits in hand, prepared to render assistance.

In shock and with tears of anxiety, Danica related to the captain of the tomb squad that she hadn't seen him enter into the tomb opening, but she had heard what sounded like a thud. She called out for Jackson and waited briefly for a reply as she remembered he would be meticulously filming. But no answer. Desperation in her voice, she called out once more. Again, she received no answer.

Fearing the worst, Danica called for members of the crew, who were nearby, quickly summoning them to her side, Responding, they each lit their torches and descended into the tomb to find and render assistance to their professor.

There, in the flickering light from their torches, they found him, some said lying with his battered and bloodied head across a sarcophagus, aside the image of the deceased persons who had been reclining on top of the funeral box all the many centuries since their funerary rights had been administered, only then to be lost in the timeless eternity or was it the infinity of the Etruscan afterlife.

With the archeological crew having gone down inside the rooms that made up the tomb, the commander of the tomb guards remained outside with Danica. He queried her and a few others of her team trying to render help to her. She pressed the others if perhaps Dr. Alioto lost his footing in the tomb entrance tripping over a rain-wet stone leading into the entrance and then fell forward and hit his head on the sarcophagus, his body helplessly falling head first into the dark void filling the tomb. There he had come to rest next to the deceased Etruscans' sculpted stone bodies displayed in their repose over countless centuries atop the ancient sarcophagus box.

But then grumbling to himself, the commander suddenly became disobliging, seeming to take a contrary tactic. In a change of view point he speculated that perhaps the good professor might, instead, have been intentionally pushed head-first down into the rooms of this particular tomb by someone among them who perhaps bore a grudge. The officer waited for a response from those above-ground members of the archaeological team, especially Danica, its now presumed leader. In silence, Danica watched the commander remove his strapped-in over-the-shoulder telephone. In line with his duty, he was punching out what she presumed to be a series of official telephone numbers, either calling for more officers from his command or other police jurisdictions.

Within a short time, joining the commander and the ambulance crew, two official-looking cars from other jurisdictions arrived. One carried the coroner, judging from his death-like look and his long white coat.

The police commander—the uniformed person with the most stars on his shoulder and the most medals on his shirt, was continuing to act in charge.

Meanwhile, Bernard was seen disappearing into the gaping entrance of a tomb, two tombs removed. But not before the police captain called after him. Bernard looked frightened and froze.

Among the folks from the conference, some could be heard whispering to one another, citing Bernard's rudeness at the conference, accusing Jackson of stealing his findings, commenting as they did about his antagonistic tone, as if they were a jury convicting Bernie of the murder of Jackson Alioto.

Meanwhile, two deputies were commandeering Bernie and escorting him to the commanding presence of the Carabiniere police captain. It wasn't long before Danica heard the Italian words for tests and possible arrest, and Bernard was disappearing into a police van. Soon the vehicle was seen leaving the site. Danica called out after him, but all she received in return was a cut-short wave of Bernard's hand as a police officer arm pulled it back to administer handcuffs. And that was the last she saw of her brief amor, the handsome curly-haired student named Bernard.

CHAPTER ELEVEN

Later

The Carabiniere Orvieto Police Headquarters

Uniforms and badges, patrol cars and flashing lights were all Danica could see and cope with as she confronted the news from the captain that Jackson was confirmed dead and she was now a widow.

She went with the captain to the Carabiniere administrative station which was, as were other municipal offices, near the Orvieto train station. All Danica was thinking about as she caught a view of a train leaving the station was that she yearned to escape this town in the same way that this sleek train was doing, and it was picking up speed, a speed she coveted as she visually followed the train in its escape into an elsewhere somewhere that represented her freedom from what must be the facts of the day.

In a professional manner, and in understandable English, Captain Benito Valisco, she now saw as she read his official nametag, explained politely to Danica, "We will be holding student Bernard Monterossa until we can check the back of Dr. Alioto's coat for evidence proving that the student pushed him…an act which he denies," the commander appended and went on, "But if he did so push, there'll be hand print evidence on the back of the American's jacket. That will be sufficient evidence for us to charge him with the crime.

CHAPTER TWELVE

Jackson's Wishes

Soon afterward, Dorothy Overman and Kip called from Berlin to Orvieto to express their sorrow to Danica at hearing of Jackson's demise.

In her most concerned voice, Dorothy, holding back tears, said to Danica when she answered her cell, that she and Kip were shocked at the news that they had just been given by the Max Plank staff. "Danica Dear, they've just told us. How Tragic it all is. We're so sorry to hear and, of course, we are concerned for your well-being."

Danica thanked them for calling and then, losing control, she broke down in tears. Recovering fairly quickly, she apologized for losing control of her emotions.

Kip tried to calm her down by asking if she was planning a memorial service for Jackson. "You know, the American Embassy in Rome—which I can notify on your behalf—has a plan for returning the deceased to America."

"Yes, the Plank people have advised me of that benefit, but Jackson re-wrote his last instructions just two weeks ago. He had become so enamored with the Etruscans and their lifestyle that he decided that if anything ever happened to him, he wanted his ashes distributed across an Etruscan burial ground. Along this line, I must find a crematorium here in this Catholic country. I'm thinking of doing that here in Orvieto."

Dorothy then asked, 'Danica, have you thought about your life ahead? I mean—"

"—Oh, yes, briefly, of course. I realize life goes on, and I'm thinking about what I must do. I need to organize my thoughts...you know...for my future."

Kip asked, "Is there anything Dorothy and I can do to help you right now?"

Danica quickly replied, "Yes, there is, Kip. One of Jackson's and my students, Bernard Monterossa by name, Is being held by the police in Orvieto on suspicion of having been somehow involved in Jackson's death, which I know he is not."

"Is he Italian?"

"Yes, with—and with Etruscan lineage, or so he claims, along with a lot more information he has compiled about the Etruscans."

Kip replied, "We'll try to get an Italian attorney to get him free of police custody."

"Oh, that'd be wonderful. He has a lot of compiled information about the story of the Etruscans which, at first blush, seems a bit far out, but he claims documentation, and I'd like to pursue his findings with him.

"As to the League?"

"Yes, of nations and the other one."

"The 12?"

"The 13."

Dorothy asked, "What about the archaeologist from New Mexico?"

"Stuart Sweet. Yes, he's quite interesting. He brought one of his students with him, and it seems he has a major find among the Anasazi, that is, if it proves out."

Kip said, "That's exciting."

"He's planning a dinner with his students—there are nine, I think, in his retirement home overlooking Big Sur, at which he and his students will vote on whether or not to release the news of their finding, assuming that tests come back favorable, or so I understand."

Dorothy said, "It'll be fun to follow the developments.

"Yes, Stuart will be inviting all of us to come to his dinner party and vote, that is…if we vote to go public with our finds about the Etruscans and the Anasazi."

CHAPTER THIRTEEN

The Two Sexes

In a custom of yesteryear, arrangements between members of the two sexes were arranged by their respective tribal matriarchs for purity of possible offspring. However, In our world of today, when two adults of opposite sexual orientation meet and, either slowly or quickly, interact with each other, nurturing their mutual interest in the other, a chemistry of human emotions, mysteriously special, seems to take place. It may occur instantaneously, perhaps limited to promptly acknowledged feelings or else, like a late spring rain, come slowly yet deliberately upon the scene. But once it arrives, both parties share the welcoming moisture of common feelings developing between them.

For our story's two central characters, each so destined to share an interest in the other, even at their respective ages. And why not? Archaeologists are like peoples they study, are modern human beings, each with personal human emotions. In their own earth-bound time, they are here now, not back there among "those who have gone before," those whom they have diligently studied—and still do—embedded in each of their respective, yet very different, academic careers.

In an ensuing series of normal dialogues, a couple far apart chronologically in their respective fields, will tenderly and eventually explore the other's likes and dislikes, the values and lives of their respective parents and how they may have met back there in time. From there, it's on to their own selfish likes and dislikes—movies, books, travel, spiritual feelings.

Seldom though in this dialogue of souls, does the subject of ancient prehistoric peoples, of ancestors or those of intellectual interest, enter into this delicate exploration of feelings, likes, values, and moreover the possible future of their lives together should they decide to travel along with each other in a common direction.

Coming from out of the past, the future shines its light and suggests that the wisdom of maturity will surely guide the couples' record of earlier years and help them sculpt a future together. But how can such conversations effectively span a total of 4,000 bracketed years of prehistory, history, academic papers, excavation reports, and scientific studies, each well-conceived and professionally presented? How can and will two academics' respective pasts shape their future together? How indeed?

* * *

Dr. Stuart Sweet has aggressively studied the American Ancestral Puebloans, the prehistory peoples so re-named to be popularly and politically correct, instead of the Anasazi—characterized by the present-day Navajo as "they who are not us." For well more than a century, the ancestral sites of many different but aligned cultures have been popular tourist attractions located throughout the American Southwest, mainly scattered throughout New Mexico and Arizona.

Danica Alioto is an archaeologist who has devoted her second career to the study of the pre-Roman Etruscans, who pre-date by a couple thousand years the New World Ancestral Puebloans. These two dedicated archaeologists were perhaps destined to meet at an archaeology conference in present-day Italy. The never-married Stuart, always charting his own course but now, in later life, decrying an emotional loneliness in his decades-long career as an academic. So, at this meeting of minds, it was Etruscans versus the Ancestral Puebloans that filled the academic dialogue between those in attendance and especially these two. Romantic? Not as in Hollywood scripts. Yet more serious, not fleeting, but tender, as in their lives in what has become today's world.

Danica has been recently widowed in a tragic incident in an Etruscan tomb causing the death of her late husband, Dr. Jackson Alioto. One person questioned was the student, Bernard Monterossa, who had been telling about unorthodox revelations surrounding the pre-Roman Etruscans

* * *

Letter Exchange

In his college days, Stuart Sweet's academic studies had focused on archaeology in related fields of science relating to the Anasazi. But he had struggled through one required literature course just to try to find out about the field. He recalled the professor talking about the subject of romance in literature, which had arisen from the custom of writing letters, which he was not Stuart's strong point, although he did excel in the task of writing his field reports on archaeological excavations, as well as required papers for newsletters and academic journals in his chosen field.

While attending the memorial service honoring Dr. Jackson Alioto, Stuart's thoughts bounced from the tragic incident to curiosity about Danica He was trying to compose a letter to her, beginning with the fact that they had been back-to-back speakers at the podium just days before at the Max Planck Conference in Tarquinia.

Taking out a crumpled notebook from his case, he found a blank page and began:

To: Dr. Danica Alioto:

May I express to you my deepest condolences for the untimely death of your husband, Jackson. It was indeed a tragedy.

I feel certain your late dear husband would want you and me to continue the spirit of the conference for the benefit of all the students who signed up, as well as to fulfill our commitment to the Max Planck organization. I wish to suggest that you and I do so in a paper about our respective fields of expertise—you for the Etruscans and me for the Anasazi. Perhaps we can outline a comparison of the traits of two different cultures, including habits in ceremonial events.

We can talk more this evening about your interest in doing so.

But, at some point, I must tell you about the discovery my students have uncovered in the Anasazi's Pueblo Bonita ruins in Chaco Canyon. I will cherish your thoughts about this mind-bending discovery. That will likely lead us into a long discussion about our two unique discoveries—the Etruscans and their13-member League and my student's discovery of…well, the document one of my students discovered in the Grand Kiva. After our discussions, we must decide what to do with each of these breakthrough bits of information, as in my opinion, they are each earthshaking for our profession. I need your thoughts, Danica. Please agree to help me.

Yours sincerely,
Stuart Sweet

At the conclusion of the service, Stuart tore the page from his notebook, folded it, stood and took the few steps toward Danica, handing the page to her. He smiled and turned away, somewhat embarrassed.

* * *

Danica had been discretely surveying her new male interest—Stuart—sitting across the room from her. He had once looked over at her, smiling a bit, she noticed right away. Indeed, he was noticeably masculine, she had to admit. His image struck a familiar response, which she admitted to herself she liked. Yet there was a thing of tiredness revealed to her in the tiny wrinkles drawn across his forehead. It was, of course, those years of academic assignments, tensions, and, yes, political considerations registering on and revealed deeply in his person. Was this outward reveal so different from herself and the picture she transmitted?

Now, coming up on retirement, perhaps Stuart was wondering, as was Danica, what had it all meant—all those students, all those scientific, hot and dirty excavations, all those professional papers, all those student lectures, reading all those student papers, grading them—considering what was appropriate to award. She recalled, trying not to think about it, but she did anyway—couldn't help it, she acknowledged. The academic drill flooded her mind once again: the image of students in class, in conference, raising the oft-asked questions--she as a teacher humble, too humble, aggressive, too aggressive to become a teacher, a personality suitable for a researcher, for an archaeologist deciding where to dig and what to look for—traits needed for a good academic person coveting tenure at some university somewhere, overseas or back home.

Then there were all those meticulously prepared and, to be frank, rather dry talks delivered to others gathered in the typical conference lecture hall somewhere. These days, this day, this moment, looking back, where was the satisfying thread? No, it was rather the tightly woven warp of a satisfactory career? It was supposed to be there. But was it? For him? For her? She vowed that she must find out, for her sake in their upcoming Etruscan-like relationship, whatever that might or might not be or even lead to.

CHAPTER FOURTEEN

Days of Speculation

During the precious days of their rather atypical relationship (accelerated to those accustomed to the snails' progress of academic affairs), Stuart charged his later-in-life female interest to match his out-of-mind experiences. He asked her to tell him one of her recently-learned stories of having been among the even more ancient Etruscans who had lived in many parts of Italy centuries-ago.

Reflecting, Danica began her response, beginning with a series of experiences getting in the mind of those Etruscan artists who painted their artwork on the walls of tombs. "I can't personally comment on their art, but D. H. Lawrence a hundred years ago does so. She took from her case a book and read, "The English author said that the Etruscans, through their art, had a profound belief in life and its continuance, which is evident in the art displayed on the walls of their tombs."

To Stuart, she continued to quote D. H. Lawrence writing from the 1920s, "Now we know nothing about the Etruscans except what we find in their tombs. There are references to them in Latin writers. But of first-hand knowledge we have nothing except what the tombs offer. So, to the tombs we must go: or to the museums containing the things that have been rifled from the tombs. Myself, the first time I consciously saw Etruscan things, in the museum at Perugia, I was in-

stinctively attracted to them. The tombs seem so easy and friendly...
it must be partly owing to the peculiar charm of natural proportion
which is in all Etruscan things of the unspoiled, unromanticized
centuries ago. There is a simplicity, combined with a most peculiar,
free-breasted naturalness and spontaneity in the shapes and movements of the underworld walls and spaces, that at once reassures the
spirit. The Greeks sought to make an impression, and Gothic still
more seeks to impress the mind, The Etruscans, no."

Lawrence says that, "Through their art, they had a profound belief in life and its continuance which is evident in the art displayed
on the walls of their tombs."

Danica explained to Stuart, "These are my out-of-mind experiences I've gained from studying the Etruscans throughout the past
month since Jackson and I came to Italy." She then described to Stuart the most memorable and realistically visual experience was excitedly imprinted in her mind. It occurred while mesmerized, in what
she described to Stuart as a growing trance triggered by the faces of
this happy bridal couple on their wedding night, reclining and embracing on a divan. In their presence, she told Stuart, she had moved
herself toward affectionate camaraderie with the woman depicted.

Danica went on, "The bride and groom are reclining on a divan,
absorbed in the anticipated events of their wedding night ahead."
Danica told Stuart that the life-size art work had been sculpted presumably in the 6th century BC. "Staring at this couple in matrimo-
nial love," recalled by her to Stuart after she and Stuart had met, she
told him at that time of her seeing the Etruscan marriage sculpture,
Danica had readily envisioned herself as the young Etruscan bride.
Entranced in her groom's magical influence, she had quickly flashed
into the future, forecasting that her groom was to travel across the
centuries to become one of the first kings of the new kingdom of
Rome. And she, his bride, was to become his beloved queen in Ro-

man circles." Danica then recounted to Stuart how, as queen of the Romans, she would elevate all the women of Rome to achieve the status that woman of the Etruscans had risen to—a marital, sexual, and cultural equality with their men. Indeed, with all men.

Surely, she told him, given her newly gained royal status, she could find out what had happened to Jackson, that is, how he had died. The police had promptly gone into the Etruscan tomb. This new team of officers began to focus their attention on the one graduate student who had let it be known to them that Bernard had published a paper—a paper he had written about his research into the chemical makeup of the paints used by the Etruscans, their origin, and their derivation geographically, concluding that most of the paints had come from vegetables and flowers grown on the island of Sardinia. Bernard had said that he claimed to be the one with the discovery, having just returned from a summer exploration in Sardinia without either her or the team leader's presence, contrary to academic custom.

But there was a second paper, the one Bernard had made such a commotion about during the conference and which he had told her about and the motivation for his outbreak. Yet, neither she nor anyone else had told the authorities about its details.

The Italian authorities had declined to charge Bernard for the Jackson's death. As they stated in their final report, Jackson's death was caused by an accident—he had tripped on a stone in the entrance to the tomb and plunged head first down into the depths of the tomb hitting his head in a final and fatal blow on a sarcophagus displaying on its top, in true Etruscan fashion, the sculptured likes of the persons for whom the tomb had been constructed. They told her it was up to her to pursue the matter any further if she so wanted by hiring her own counsel or investigators.

"What did it matter?" She had posed this question to Stuart as they got to know each other better. Jackson was dead, and his, or his student's paper about the chemical makeup of Etruscan paints was now part of the academic record, whether it was accurate, or guesswork—well, that was up for someone someday to perform further research, if any, if ever. The idea, or his find, was either up for grabs, or for the bone yard of archaeology, waiting, ever so waiting for someone to prove it either right or wrong, or for it to be ignored and relegated into the bone yard of antiquity. To Stuart, she asked, "What does it matter? The acclaimed beautify of Etruscan art is destined for its earned place in the annals of beauty and creativity to endure forever and ever. "

The two then bantered, describing, extolling, comparing, judging, rating, wanting to write ethical papers on the respective merits of each of their respective early culture specialties, one much earlier on the timeline of our species—the peoples we are today, the people and their universities for which Stuart and Danica were employed and from which they would retire. And then do what with their lives?

Surprising Danica, Stuart asked if Etruscans retired? Danica returned his serve, bouncing the question back yet still within the lines of mutual affection. For there was no other direction to go. And they laughed together. As pupils. As teachers. As moderns, still, each wondering what the real answers would be for their coming lives. Surely together. And they hugged the hug of togetherness—two as one—facing their future together.

But what was to be the future for those leaving their footprints in the sands of time? Career times two. The question remaining as unanswered as the interpretation of the Etruscan written language— read right to left instead of left to right, read strange characters not knowing the true—only guessed—sounds, let alone the true meaning as later to be spoken in our language terms, yet not in their terms because the symbols obviously had meaning, as they kept writing the characters, one after the other with the characters appearing similar to certain modern-day writing, though undecipherable so as to satisfy the academics who study such matters. Still, no sentences, no paragraphs, no titles, just inverted letters, on and on, without the horizons, the hills and valleys of thought.

Stuart interrupted to say to Danica that the Anasazi had only their art as they had expressed it so frequently on rock art, no letters of some strange alphabet, no characters, just rock art. Yet of necessity they needed to communicate with one another, including the peer pressure to listen to and heed what their powerful and frightening shaman was telling them about when to plant their crops, when to harvest the bounty, and what to stand in awe of in the natural world, those unexplained phenomena they held in awe surrounding them day and night from out of the heavens, both shining down on them and then hidden by the clouds. It was always as if those forces from the heavens were immediate and maybe any minute might descend upon them. Perhaps the forces of heaven might be enhancing the danger of empowering them with the electric energy.

Danica, at Stuart's urging, went on to characterize—in a contrasting portrayal—the Etruscans, "In what is today the nation of Italy, and back before the Romans, they were building tombs into almost every hilltop, for it might seem to today's observer that their lives were consumed with the taming of death." He went on to repeat a familiar and oft-said funerary quote, "Oh, Death, where is thy sting?" He added a deep query to her, "Taming? How can you—I mean they—could they tame death?"

She mulled over his question, and then told him, "I believe from my research and the research of others—and this may seem extreme to you..."

"...Try me..."

She did, "It is evident to me that the major mission in the life of every Etruscan was to regard death as a continuance of their life, and to so treat it through their funerary practice of building tombs and bid a deceased person a fond farewell by a tomb so designed that it represented the deceased's life and her or his surroundings, as painted and depicted within the walls of the tomb. In the tomb they would bid a good- bye to the deceased on the way to another world, their visit there enhanced by the depictions on the walls of the tomb, many times suggesting the passage of the deceased, and his or her happiness with the journey and their next destination.

"And?" He waited and then asked, "And how do you draw such weird conclusions?"

Danica responded, "Just look at each of their sarcophagi."

"What do they show you?"

"People sitting atop their burial chamber, happy, smiling, ready and anxious to move on."

"Your imagination is running wild."

"To be a good archaeologist, your imagination must be so empowered."

"While I agree with you, not many in academia will fall in line on that point."

Danica grew quiet; then bubbled with, "Just think, Stuart, how many students we teach each year, and they each go out into the world—maybe not every one of them, our graduates, go on into academia, and perhaps not into teaching but into research."

"Go on."

"How many—count them—are in research?"

"I don't know. No one tabulates the totals, so far as I know." Stuart thought for a moment and then suggested "But there are probably hundreds, yes...likely thousands when you take in all the colleges and universities in the world."

"Exactly." She came down hard on her ensuing comment, "Given the questions still haunting us about the Etruscans and your Ana-sazi, sooner or later, someone among these new students-turned into dedicated researchers is going to add to the body of knowledge, increasing what we know and what we suspect went on, so many years ago. Don't you agree with me?"

"Yes of course, that's why we don't excavate all the sites we have today—we leave a lot for generations to come, for them to explore with their new techniques, and their new equipment and instruments. Yes, just think of all the answers that await us in the decades to come."

She added, "And in this decade. Here goes: I mean, for clarification, I mean the decade we're now in."

"Suppose so. Yes, sure, why not?"

Danica waited for his conclusions to sink in and then underlined them: "So, if I tell you about a research finding, or rather an expand-ed-upon idea—"

"—Substantiated?"

"Decide for yourself."

"You're on."

"Here goes: My student—:

"Now wait just a minute!"

"No, I want to lay it all out for you, before you begin your usual critical peer review...promise me?"

Reluctantly, waiting a moment, Stuart nodded.

Danica said, "The Etruscan League."

"Twelve cities, wasn't it, as I recall."

"Thirteen, including Orvieto."

Danica said, "So follow me now—"

"—To the ends of the earth."

Danica laughed and then threw a kiss toward Stuart. "So, my student reported to me about his research into the Etruscan League."

"This is the same person who you think...who you say... may have pushed your husband down into an Etruscan tomb, causing him—"

"Same guy. That is, if he did, but he didn't.

"The one you were attracted to?"

"Briefly...

Stuart repeated, "Briefly," and chuckled as if everyone knew what 'briefly' could and probably did suggest.

"Never mind. We're academics here, right?"

"In your brief affair, or with the Etruscans?"

"Damn it all, Stuart, let me tell you Bernard's findings." Danica grew dogmatic. "That's the subject, that's what we're talking about right this minute."

"Just want to know the players on the field, that's all."

"So, now you know."

"And now I want to know about his research...please, the research you are clearly defending?"

"He found a translation from Etruscan into Phoenician and then into Greek, so we now have found out pretty much what the Etruscans were saying about their League, and its powers, its direction, as well as its on-going governance."

"That's a major breakthrough, sounds like, I'd say."

"You'd say right!"

"So, what are the answers, our new knowledge, I mean?"

Danica replies, "First I must tell you about a tidbit of information concerning Woodrow Wilson."

"Oh, come on, Danica...you mean...?"

"Yes, him, that's the man..."

"And now your research is going to tell me that he was an Etruscan, a pioneer of his people, and later became one of the first kings of Rome."

"I'm not going to tell you any of that dribble."

"Good."

"What I am going to tell you is that my student Bernard's further research gave him a tiny look into Wilson's bio which is where Wilson advanced his idea for the League of Nations."

"Yikes! You're kidding me. Danica, we don't have time for this sort of thing."

"That's what my student found."

"Says he found...where's his documentation?"

"Says it's a confidential source...locked away in some vault...at some Italian location...I mean, a well-known location that in the past has yielded a lot of information...most of which has been substantiated."

"By whom?"

"A few in the Italian academic community."

"Found by some starving student from Naples wanting a scholarship to a university in Milan or...?"

Danica smiled and said sweetly to Stuart, "But suppose it's true?"

"Like the canals on Mars, to be augmented with a quote from one of their canal boatmen speaking to us in unaccented English." Stuart paused, adding, "Danica, you and I are sworn by oath to deal in facts, not creative fiction."

"I repeat, 'Suppose it's true?'"

"Then we must try to prove it, substantiate it so that it passes peer review." Stuart added, "And with verifiable documentation."

"Well, then you can chase this further bit of startling information to your heart's content. Here it is: how many American colonies were there?"

Stuart was quick with, "Thirteen."

"And how many cities formed the Etruscan League?"

"Thirteen, counting Orvieto."

Danica allowed the ensuing silence to sink in, thus underlining it for emphasis.

Stuart scoffed, "I suppose your student's going to have found the trip receipt for Jefferson's trip to Tarquinia that will verify Jefferson's find, he having talked to a dozen of the local Etruscans."

"Not quite, but something like that, as good, or so my student claims."

"And you buy all the what if?" she asked, adding, "There's an entire body of knowledge out there that nobody has yet discovered, and you and I are about to do so. It has been written in a strange and unique language, reading from right to left, as the Etruscans wrote their stories and thoughts."

"Maybe upside down, as well," Stuart suggested with a wink toward Danica.

She responded with, "You're being silly."

The two laughed together, both on an idea and on the unity of their growing affection for each other, no matter if they were sharing such a far distant topic from an ancient time.

"Sobering," Stuart suggested, "Let's come back to the reality of the 21st century."

"Why not the reality of the 5th century BC?"

"What is this: a game of 'Choose Your Century'?"

"Yes, in which to live and be a part of—back then with a totally different culture, as we experience the feelings and emotions of those many who have gone before."

"Okay," Stuart said, "I'll pick the 18th Century and the American Revolution."

Diana added, "That's when Thomas Paine wrote his empire-shaking book, shaking the staid old British Empire."

"And heating up the American Revolution, going from simmering to boiling."

"Yes, and do you know this about him?"

"What's that?"

"Paine began writing the book in England while he was staying in a hotel in the south—Lewes was the town. He was there trying to resolve a list of personal matters—debts, for example—before he would be able to book passage to the American Colonies."

"I have the feeling you're going to embellish this story."

"No, just relate it—"

"—From your student?"

"Yes, from his research; you see, he was a history minor."

"More of your fluffy pillow talk?"

"No, this is straight-forward history."

"So, he was in this hotel…and then…?"

"Paine needed to go off to Italy on one of his many quests to resolve another of his debts. After boating across the English Channel, he booked a carriage ride south along the old Roman Road." In response to observing Stuart's raised eyebrows, Danica went on to tell him about the Roman Road and its route through Pietrasanta, Siena and still more Italian towns. When Paine reached the Tuscany area and the old Etruscan town of Volterra, in the course of settling his debt, he learned about the 13 cities that were members of the Etruscan League. She explained the League's existence in those ancient times but also about its role in trying to counteract the burgeoning Roman city-state with its insidious empire-like ambitions—much the same as, at the time, the English Empire that Paine wanted his beloved 13 colonies to break away from."

Stuart said, "So Paine went back to his little hotel in the south of England and kept on writing?"

"No, now free of all his debts, he was able to book passage to the New World to Philadelphia where he finished his book. After finding a publisher, Paine began to distribute his book, entitled "Common

Sense," among the many patrons he had befriended in the popular City Tavern which was in the heart of the Revolutionary spirit that was gripping the City of Brotherly Love."

Stuart said, sort of shaking his head in advanced disbelief, "And the idea of the 13- member Etruscan League—that's the idea Bernard was telling us that those centuries ago inspired our own 13 Colonies to unite and form the Continental Congress, what later became the American Republic."

"You got it."

Stuart, trying to stifle a scoff said, "But you and he are dead serious, aren't you?"

Danica smiled, gave him a quick kiss on the cheek, "Let me explain a bit to you. This morning I had the most amazing experience. As you know, I've never put shades on my windows because I've liked to look out and see across the treetops, giving me the feeling I'm as free as the birds I see. You see, I feel I am above it all, at least at times like this morning. And this morning the full moon in a white bright whiteness shown through the window glass…. It was about 6:30 AM, awakening me with its brilliance. Its beautiful whiteness was shining at me through all the many exciting fall colors of a liquid amber tree with its red and crimson, casting light on all the reds and their palette of shades while triggering in me all sorts of imaginative trains of thought, like it was…well…a railroad switchyard as one idea led to another track and more trains and more tracks of all types—passenger and freight were all mixed together from steam to diesel. Then the thoughts flooded my mind as if a drought of ideas was being swamped by an overhead river of rain.

"And what were your thoughts?"

"Suppose, I said to myself, and only to myself, what if much of what we know or think we know is not accurate, not right on, not substantiated by the truth, by science, by documentation from valued

72

sources? What if we are really back in the early times of knowledge, searching for our status—you know, our position in time, searching for why we are here, and where we are going? And for what sorts of possible personal rewards?"

"And what did you conclude?"

"That an artist's canvas—maybe an entire gallery—of revelations exist out there awaiting us if we know where and how to look, how to ask the right questions, how to explore each and every topic we imagine to be important to our understanding of life, of the universe, of spirituality, even, yes even of history, and certainly to your and my findings so far in our respective fields of archeology."

Danica paused and added still more thoughts to her silent and somewhat bewildered listener, "Stuart, there are new telescopes probing outer space, examining planets in our own universe and beyond."

He nodded and contributed, "Yes, they are big and very expensive, their design and launch being funded by several countries' governments."

"And they're each looking for something that suggests signs of life—not people waving at us, not people building sinister space ships to attack us, like in "War of the Worlds," but simply traces or hints of some sort of biology, a trace even of the chemistry that is essential for life, simply for the elementary building blocks of life." Danica went on, "And what if these signs of life are really actual forms of intelligent life, and these new forms have devised some sort of culture, some sort of government that is ever so unlike anything on this planet? Perhaps it will be based on, let's say, programming the genes of babies so that they are destined to behave in a predetermined manner of conformity so thorough and complete that for these baby beings no education of such offspring is ever required— the newborn just live and die and in the process of their being, they conform to some sort of predetermined norm?"

"To what the Dear Leader specifies. And who might be this Dear Leader?"

"A mutation perhaps."

"Yes, you know, every so often—and regularly—fruit flies mutate. So, in these new worlds out there, the folks—whatever you want to call them—mutate, and a leader is created, whose directions and edicts everybody is programmed to follow."

Stuart reacted, "How horrible! But even in our world aren't we today getting mutated leaders who don't follow the expected, the traditional, the norm, the story of history, but rather counter it, ignore it, and try to mold society to their personal satisfactions."

"But how," Danica wondered, "would we know when one of these Mutations came along?"

Stuart speculated, "Their mesmerizing charisma would be projected across a swatch of the obedient population and thereafter dominate peoples' behaviors."

Danica fretted, "My dear father would say—and always did to me on matters of this sort—that you needed to look below the surface of what a person is trying to say, whether it is some important news or just an unfounded rumor.

"What did tour father do in academia?"

She replied, "Oh, he wasn't in academia; my father was in the military and we were stationed in the Canal Zone."

"Panama."

Danica nodded and went on, "Back before the country of Panama took over running the Canal."

"Jimmy Carter gave the Canal Zone back to the Panamanians, as I recall."

"Not before my father, name was Luther, after Martin, you know—Lt. Colonel, his rank at retirement—had his say as to the history of the canal—that is, the French—and the color yellow."

"For the fever?"

"You got it."

"Stuart protested, "But what's that—"

Danica interrupted, "—His credo was, and he emphasized it to me so many times that I will never forget his counter-military admonition, which succinctly stated was: 'Always question, never take things for granted. In the Army,' he philosophized, 'Always follow orders, but always in your own mind ask yourself questions as to the wisdom of the orders, who was giving them, and how you would say it or write it differently.'"

"And that's what you're advocating for the two of us when it comes to the Etruscans…"

"…And everything else."

"For example?"

Danica enumerated, "Take the yellow fever."

"A plague upon construction, wasn't it?"

"Yes, but everyone's knowledge of it went back hundreds of years. People believed that the yellow fever (and malaria) were spirits that emanated from the miasma that, at dusk and on into the night, rose up from marshes and stagnant ponds and brought disease and illness when you breathed in the stale pungent air. So, they remained in their houses after dusk. That is, until a young chemist began to investigate. His finding that the awful mosquito carried the disease and passed it on to you when it bit you—well, that was heresy into peoples' beliefs, and the young man was ridiculed. It was an isolated treatment for many years until several others came up with the same conclusion. And the light was turned on, but it took a long time really for people in general to accept this new solution to Yellow Fever and for the Panama Canal, under American leadership and finance, to actually get constructed."

"Now we get vaccinated against Yellow Fever."

Danica smiled and proclaimed, "Isn't science wonderful!"

"And you mentioned your father's rant against the French."

"Yes, you see the reputation of the French leader was deeply ingrained in the French mind—and consequently in the minds of everyone in Panama and the Western World, especially after he had built the Suez Canal in Egypt. Everyone just automatically assumed he would get the job done in an equal amount of time and cost. French country people bought stock in the French Panama Canal, bet their life savings on its success. But as the years went by and the costs piled up along with a few piles of dirt and some hospitals to treat the insipid yellow fever—and let me tell you the French didn't install screens on their newly-built hospitals' windows, so it was a mass invitation for the mosquitos to invade and bite patients and the staff, spreading the dreaded disease to all the new arrivals from France and elsewhere.

Finally, the French leader realized the task was over his head. He soon acknowledged that locks had to be built to get the ships up and over the high backbone of the Isthmus from the Atlantic Ocean to the Pacific Ocean, and back again."

"And Teddy Roosevelt"

"Organized a coup to grab the province of Panama away from the South American country of Columbia. Panama would then be diplomatically recognized. Its newly appointed diplomats would quickly strike a deal for an American zone across the Isthmus. With no one to challenge, the Americans could now start to build the canal with the appropriate locks that would sooner or later complete the waterway linking the Caribbean and the Pacific."

"That's what you mean by always asking question and not be afraid of endorsing a radical set of beliefs, even beginning with the new hypothesis?" Stuart grew skeptical, maybe even pouting as he hesitatingly asked, "But this graduate student of yours? What's his story? I mean, you were attracted to him...right?"

Danica's reaction caused Stuart to apologize, "Sorry, I'm being too personal."

"But not unrealistic. Yes, Bernard might have killed...."

"Intentionally?" Danica hesitated. "Well, sort of." She waited, then went on, "Let me tell you his story, and then you decide."

"I'm no judge and jury. Even if we are talking about archaeology."

"Try."

"Tell me then."

"He was born in Italy."

"Where?"

"On the Roman Road in the little Medieval town of Camiore."

"The Roman Road?"

Danica explained, "The road from the Vatican to England, across the channel by boat, of course. It went through Siena and most towns, including where my student was born and grew up. But something happened to him early in life, or so he told me." She narrated to Stuart the story. "My student told me that in his school one day an archaeologist from a big university in Milan came and talked to the students. In the course of his lecture, the professor made a joke about the Etruscans—said the Roman Road was built on one of their roads, at least as far as north of Siena—that's where the Etruscans towns were fewer."

"And?"

"My student's curiosity was triggered and he began to look into the stories about the Etruscans. First, he asked his father a lot of questions."

"Such as?"

"Such as: are we descended from an Etruscan family?"

"Bernard's father wouldn't know…that's for sure don't you think? I mean after all…all those years, centuries…"

"It's not completely out of the question, you'll have to admit. And his father said he thought so."

"I'm just sure Ancestry.com would know…give me a break! Come on, Danica!"

"Please hear me out."

"I will." He appended, "Of course."

Danica continued, "My student's father talked a lot about the Etruscans to the point that Bernard began to believe his father's statement that their family were descendant from an Etruscan family. His father even suggested a particular family name, which I've forgotten. Imbued with his father's strong belief, Bernard soon became convinced of the story's authenticity.

"And then what happened?"

"Well, the worst of things took place. Bernard told me how he had repeated the story to his new archaeological professor—"

"—Guess who?"

"—You've got it!"

"And your student's grade suffered?"

"Through the floor. Jackson told him he was on thin ice—really thin ice and to forget it, for it was just not even in the realm of statistical possibility."

Stuart said softly and slowly, dragging out the word, "Motive. But tell me, Danica, what is your attraction to these long-ago Etruscans. I mean, if you are going to devote a good deal of your time researching a culture, studying a people and their art, artifacts, and all that, you must have some sort of deep attraction for them. Perhaps as you study them, you've developed a kinship of sorts with them, like I do for the Anasazi of the Four Corners."

"So, please tell me, Stuart, what is this Anasazi attraction of yours?"

CHAPTER FIFTEEN

Their Conversation

Thoughtfully he responded to Danica, "To me these ancient people led a most interesting and challenging life, exploring the area of the Earth which they found themselves occupying, building their multiple-story pueblos, living their lives, infatuated as they were with their surroundings, their pristine natural world, raising their children, attentive to their shamans, growing their crops, managing to survive many years when there was little or no rainfall in their high desert climate.

Danica thought for a moment, organizing her emotions before she replied. "Let me tell you about my imagined and real tie to the Etruscans. As I look at their tombs, study their art—much of it painted on the walls of their tombs in what was at that time brilliant colors—I envision myself living in their hilltop towns, traveling their roads—that is, before the Romans took over their lands…well, I have come to enumerate their traits and compare their lives and their societies with ours here today in what we call our modern world.

"Go on, please."

Danica began what Stuart rapidly came to regard as a freshman class lecture to be entitled "Etruscans 101." First, in a mental embrace that reminded her of what she had come to re-live as an Etruscan show of affection between two adult individuals. "It's all so day-by-day normal with them," she began.

Stuart waited.

Collecting herself, Danica tried to organize her obvious and outward show of emotions about the people with whom she had spent her recent and rather new academic career studying. Slowly she proclaimed, "To me, they always appear to be happy, to be content with their lot, to be fond of each other, clearly not allowing anything disruptive to come in their way. Just look at the poses they exhibit on their sarcophagi in their tombs. In life and in death the Etruscans were happy, fond of each other. Look at the expressions on their faces. They visited tombs and welcomed back the deceased on the reminder days of their having passed away. To them, the deceased were still with them, still existing, representing a continuance of life from birth through the endless death. In other words, those who had died were still really alive, at least in spirit."

"And what would that sort of life be like?" Stuart thought she would have addressed her class, her students—asking them to imagine life without a burden of rules, laws, retribution, police...society controlling them. They had their warriors who fought when they had to in order to protect, but they didn't go looking for wars, for battle, for retaliation. He asked almost to himself, "What would life be without intrusive government, without taxes, without laws, without courts, without judges, without punishment?"

Danica returned his speculations, "Freedom of movement, freedom of thought...."

"An acceptable form of anarchy."

"Yes, but freedom, no controls over activities, movements, speech...."

"Is that what your Etruscans enjoyed?"

Danica said slowly, "I believe it is something along that line."

"But you don't know?"

"Yes, I do."

"But you and I can't go back and be one of them and live with them and experience their lives as a culture...can we?"

"No need to ask an archaeologist such a question, is there?"

In reply, Danica rummaged around in her library and came up with an artistic booklet. Handing it to him, she said as she gestured at the cover picture, "See the expression on this Etruscan woman's face. This is a sculpture of her. Look at it for a full minute and imagine being with her in real life. Imagine your conversation with her. Imagine her thoughts being expressed to you...intimately. Imagine her telling you of her contentment with her society, with her friends, with life around her."

"Okay, I'm doing that as I look at her picture."

"Think of her facial gestures to you, maybe a wink, maybe a deeper, more meaningful smile from what she displays in her picture, or maybe even a scowl if you say something she disagrees with."

"Would she slap my face?"

"I doubt it, but just maybe..."

Stuart nodded, waited in a thinking silence. Time went by. Eventually, after he had done as instructed, he reported to Danica, "She talked to me, told me about her life and the life of her community."

Danica nodded her acknowledgement. There was silence between them. After a while Danica asked, "Why do we think of the Etruscans as being somehow tied to the Romans?" Danica paused and added, "I mean I think of the Etruscans as having developed their own unique culture and way of life. And not just yielding to the Romans who eventually took over and one day occupied all of Italy, and much more, of course."

There was silence between them, then Danica said, "Yes, the Etruscans didn't plan to fade into oblivion any more than your Anasazi planned for the European takeover of their sacred lands, their pueblos, their art."

"Right. So why did the Etruscans fade away?"

"Their time here on Earth was up."

"According to some master plan?"

"A great script in the sky above us?"

"Is that what you think?"

"Not very scientific. But, no, that is not what I think, but I do think things have a way –maybe a life of their own and follow a time-table of their own, the inherent concept of creation and cancellation, like how a human and an animal, on their own schedule, do age… and eventually pass on."

Stuart asked, "In other words, if there were internal weaknesses in their culture, then sooner or later, depending on some sort of abstract mystical timetable, they would have disappeared into the night of endless eternity?"

"That's one way of saying it."

"And you're saying that's what you believe…nothing to do with the Romans?"

Danica mused, "Trouble is, if you say the Romans never happened, then you're suggesting that the Etruscans would still be with us?"

"No, for something else would have happened in the Mediterranean area…maybe the Greeks would have taken over or the Carthaginians, or some group of people from central Europe, maybe the French or the Germans, would have filled the void, for clearly, after almost a millennium, your Etruscans weren't going anywhere geographically, leaving the area ripe for somebody else to have taken over."

* * *

The Kick-Off

Danica said, "In the Beginning—when was that? One scientist claims it was during the three minutes after the Big Bang only a few billion years later, as the story unfolds, folks somewhat like us walked out of Africa, or maybe swam, or maybe fashioned some dugouts and crossed the intervening bodies of water to complete our species' population of the rest of the world."

Stuart added, "What became Europe and what became Asia were in their sights, but the two Americas were to come later—much, much later. Eventually they did meet up with people from Siberia crossing the Bering Land Bridge, making their way, as the many glaciers retreated, to what was to become Alaska and then Canada, to settle farther south, and I mean way south, to the tip of South America.

"Okay, so, now the human players—the homo sapiens—us were all in place, given some restless movings about, to act on their separate stages, rehearsing to play out what became their ethnic destinies, their unique DNAs cheering on their separate and peculiar roles in life on Earth."

Danica said, "You and I are professionally and emotionally concerned with only two of these rather ancient groups. First, the much earlier Etruscans in what has become Italy, and secondly, the Anasazi in a much later time, or more politically correct, the Ancestral Puebloans, of what is today the American Southwest. Their stories are told through the eyes, thoughts, findings, and experiences of we archaeologists and our eager students."

CHAPTER SIXTEEN

Earlier, Prior to Italy

Stuart's Planned Retirement Home on the California Coast

Lightning and thunder—the bolts so bold, so cracking, so frightening; the thunder so loud, so earth-shaking. Who wouldn't fear, today or who in yesteryear wouldn't seek some explanation, some reassurance for their own safety? Attention would focus on a person who could provide an explanation, spiritual guidance, a promise of protection, the comfort of believable answers? Stuart mentally saluted his Anasazi shaman.

On the upside, always, was the possibility that a discovery of his—even just one, please—of an excavation would someday prove to be earth-shaking, so to speak. Not likely, but just maybe. However, in this case, no one, however, knew about it, at least he continued to hope so. Of course, there were his students who had been with hi that late afternoon in the vast American Southwest.

But here, high above and overlooking Big Surf, Stuart was excited about going to Italy. He hoped he would be able to present his paper on the Anasazi, as he had proposed to the conference organizers.

Following his Italy trip, it would be time for his student dinner and their decisions to whether or not to make their class find public.

His sometime housekeeper Rosalita and her twin daughters,

living nearby, would prepare a feast of typical New Mexico cuisine. And then would be the vote on going public. Now, that the tests on the age of the ink on the scroll had come back from his favorite testing laboratory confirming the age of the document, Stuart allowed himself to fantasize about his future life here on the coast. It would be highlighted with speaking engagements. Yes, life would be fun, and his parents, bless their soles, would be proud.

As Professor Stuart Sweet rummaged through the accumulated clutter of his professional archaeological career, he again asked himself why he had never taken the time to organize his many field notes? It had always been this way whenever he searched for one specific file. Now that he was approaching retirement and had time—plenty of time on his hands, why had he not plunged into this seemingly simple task? Each time he went looking for a file, like this late afternoon outback in the room he planned to make into his office, he admonished himself for never having implemented a proper filing system, either at home or in his office at the university. Each of his many excavations had its own file—the accepted, and required, academic approach to documentation, making his official record keeping. That was for him, with his Ph.D. degree, the proper procedure. That is, in the event some academic challenged him or even added to the body of knowledge about a particular excavation—the findings of his dig would, of course, be cited. For that backup, he had his official narrative. Yes, a conscientious professor, such as himself, must be steeled and ready for peer challenges of a breaking media story of his newsworthy discovery.

CHAPTER SEVENTEEN

Their Find

Stuart glowed with pride as he recalled that one breakthrough and clearly unanticipated find that he and his students had come upon the last day of their summer dig. For sure, or maybe not so sure, given his having to appeal to the Faculty Union to support his retirement request in view of that one question raised—only one—but serious enough to delay the approval of his retirement application. But thanks to the Faculty Union, his retirement had finally been approved. "I mean," he said out loud to himself, "What else could they do?" Yes, that find on the dig earlier was still a secret—never officially revealed, so he and the Union assumed, only disclosed in his private personal field notes and to his students, yet unannounced to anyone else, in spite of the rumor. Where had that rumor come from? Again, Stuart searched his mind, and as in the past, again he came up with a blank.

The secret was the reason for each of his students gathering here with him sometime following his return from Italy—a reunion so to speak to review what to do, if anything, about their discovery which to this day remained a secret, or so he felt certain. At least that was what they had all agreed upon around their smoldering late-evening campfire—to meet again following Stuart's Italian Etruscan experience.

Stuart reflected on that night. They had each taken an oath to not tell anybody about their find until they could re-assemble at some point not too far in the future. The time gap had been agreed upon that night, and their final decision would be decided years hence. For that was after Stuart's scheduled retirement. They foresaw that by then he'd begin collecting his pension.

With Stuart ensconced in what was to be his small retirement home overlooking the Big Sur California coast, it was the agreed-upon date and time, one year later. They would each come, either by air into the San Jose airport and then by rental car, or driving in their own car to his house for what he expected would be a congenial dinner. Then would follow the dicey part, for the agenda was for them to review their discovery, rate their degree of excitement, reconsider and review their secrecy decision. They would vote once more as to whether or not to make public a formal announcement of their discovery, leaving their find either in the world's view or hidden away as remotely as Big Sur itself.

CHAPTER EIGHTEEN

Before Tarquinia's Museum Conference
How it Had Unfurled for Stuart

Stuart recalled how It had been on a most exciting and enchanted evening in the people-emptiness of today's northwestern New Mexico. He and his student team were preparing to wrap up their late summer excavation by covering the site with tarpaulins until the following summer. They'd hoof it back to their campsite where they would pack and then the following day drive their van back to campus. That was the moment when they had made their unexpected momentous discovery—right at the last minute, in fact.

Barely a few minutes later tempering their ensuing exuberance, they speculated about what this most unusual find meant to them and would mean to the world of archaeology; that is, if their discovery were to become public. Yes, they had agreed they must decide what to do about the find: either tell the world or keep their discovery a secret. tucked away in their minds and in their hearts. That was when, so they had reasoned and finally agreed, at least until they could think in more depth about their course of action—all nine of them, each of them, plus their professor, Dr. Stuart Sweet, of course. But not before they had launched into a full-hearted discussion around the remnants of their campfire flickering in their eyes and in their hearts in the dusk of that enchanting evening and the embers of their campfire.

For Stuart, reviewing his years of explorations in the area, it was a magical—and euphoric feeling. Like a runner's high. It was the pinnacle of his career, which was due soon to trail off into retirement.

He went over their ensuing discussion as night crept in around them. He replayed their comments, plus he revisited his thoughts, as they packed up around their campsite that last night under the stars before driving back to campus on the morrow and winding up the semester.

CHAPTER NINETEEN

Stuart's Dedicated Students

As he continued searching for his field notes, Stuart thought about the nine students on his dig. He had selected them as his best. Mentally he ran down the list, one by one, wondering where, in the year following their find, careers may have led them. Where were they living now and in what circumstances? It would all eventually be revealed after each had arrived from near and far for their special follow-up dinner meeting. This year or so interval, in anticipation of getting together again on a future night—a night way out in time in order to give them space to reflect, read, and think. They had each agreed to check in with Stuart two weeks in advance of the future meeting in order to receive their dinner invitation—but more than just dinner, it was to be a revisit to their decision to stay mum, or to reverse themselves and go public through the accepted academic channels laid out for revealing a major find on an excavation in the American Southwest.

Their discovery, as improbable as it had been, was still not disclosed—so Stuart reassured himself. Otherwise by now, someone in the university or in the media would have called him, asking for details—a headline for a news story. But that hadn't happened. The withheld experience and their find had haunted Stuart down through the agonizing months of the ensuing year. He felt certain their communal secret had also gnawed at each of his students. Or, had they instead put it aside as just another episode much as some students can overlook romps and adventures during their freewheeling student days?

But what really was this discovery? Was it a quirk or a game changer? Of course, the ongoing question was whether or not their find was authentic, a plant, a joke, or something else? As he continued to search for his field notes, Stuart once again visualized their discovery in the dusk of that late fall evening.

Early on in his teaching career as he began to observe the mental range and capabilities of students, Stuart recognized wide differences between one and another person's ability to visualize a set of circumstances and someone else's skills along the same line, that being the actual visualization of an event, whether something they saw or something out of the past as described to them in discussion or during one of his lectures. After reading an essay by a psychologist about visualization, Stuart acknowledged to himself that he had an extraordinary ability to imagine a scene in which he and others participated, one in which others played out their dramas before him, even though the scene may have existed only in his mind as a visualized episode. Imagination, he concluded, was a wonderful trait, so he looked for that aptitude in each of his students, recognizing it in varying degrees. Those were the students he chose for his special seminars. By his choice and their enthusiasm, they were the ones who had joined his dig that summer evening in Chaco Canyon.

CHAPTER TWENTY

The Discovery

Thinking back about that evening, Stuart couldn't recall which of his nine students it was who, in a last-minute final-evening playful mood, saw what appeared to be a loose rock in the side of the kiva wall and edged it a bit aside.

"Just out of curiosity," she—oh, yes...he saw her once again—a mental replay of his experience—yes, there she was...vivid...their budding artist-in-residence, Mary Ann. She had then remarked to the others that she just might sketch the contents of whatever she found there onto a blank page in her always-with-her spiral notebook.

Then, the older woman, Barbara, had come closer to help Mary Ann with the stone. Ramon stepped up to see what everyone assumed would be a small vacant gap in the kiva wall. "Unusual for a sacred kiva," Ramon had remarked as his hand gingerly invaded the opening. "What's this?" he exclaimed in surprise, as the others quickly gathered around.

With caution, his hand exploring the void, Ramon advised, "It feels like there's something rolled up inside, like a scroll, but I don't want to yank it out and possibly damage whatever it is."

He paused, thinking a moment as the others pressed forward. Then he said, "Deerskin, or whatever it is," for a moment as the others pressed forward. Then he said, "The deerskin, or whatever it is, would have been preserved in this dry high desert climate," Nods of the others came in unison.

Stuart recalled going over to the niche with his night light and shining the torch inside, then carefully grasping the edge of the item and ever-so-gently tugging at it. Soon whatever it was came just a little bit closer. Ever so carefully he continued to work it loose until the edge finally appeared out of the niche, emerging like the curious head of a turtle from out of its protective shell. Meanwhile, the class each asked in their own way, wanting to know, "What is it?"

Finally, Stuart allowed Ramon the last little tug, so that one of his students could claim the discovery. After all, wasn't that the mission of a teacher—to allow a student to discover on his or her own?

* * *

In that evening, Stuart speculated as to what was in his students' minds. What were they each thinking? Indeed, what was he thinking as Ramon puled whatever it was a little more into the fading twilight augmented by the light from the lamp.

No one had said a word. Yet their thoughts, their emotions, their anticipations were speaking loudly in the evening stillness.

Breaking their silence, Ramon had soon whispered, "I think maybe it is sort of a kind of scroll."

"That's what it is," Stuart recalled confirming to his students as Ramon began to slowly and carefully unroll the document.

"But what does it tell us, what does it show?" asked the young man Fletcher, who asked to be called Stote—the farm boy from Indiana.

More silence like when a group-in-awe admires the harvest moon at midnight. Ramon commented, "Deerskin. It feels like deerskin." He added, I've done some hunting and I know what it feels like—deerskin, I mean."

"But what are all those markings?" asked Mary Ann. "What should I draw in my sketch book? —Replicate them, I guess, wanting to be accurate."

Stuart had slowly unrolled the scroll, as they all peered at the unfamiliar markings set forth on the deerskin in what was some sort of a design or pattern.

Victor suggested, "It looks like a sketch, maybe even a building plan."

Barbara said, "I agree, but of what place?"

Victor replied, "Maybe of this place—Pueblo Bonita."

* * *

At that moment, Stuart's mind had traveled back in time to his own student days and during his first visit to Chaco Canyon. After having spent time exploring Pueblo Bonito, he had asked his archaeologist instructor, "Dr. Drake, Sir, the Anasazi must have had a plan for this place—and he had gestured at the extent of the ancient building— don't you think? Otherwise, how could they have ever built such a large multi-storied structure?"

Dr. Drake had replied, "Yes, at its peak development Pueblo Bonita rose several stories. However, no plan or drawing has ever been discovered. Pueblo Bonita was the largest building in North America until it was bypassed by an East Coast apartment in the late 1800s. But no architects or designer's plans for Pueblo Bonita or any of the other large multi-storied pueblos of the Anasazi—Mesa Verde, Hovenweep, Hopi, Laguna...and on and on...nothing...nothing even remotely resembling a set of plans has ever been found."

Stuart remembered at that point having insisted on reiterating his question for he strongly believed his idea had merit. He started again, "But they—"

"No, no one has ever discovered anything along that line. It is a good question, Stuart, but the answer is, and I repeat an absolute and profound 'nada.'"

Stuart recalled continuing to badger his instructor, "But. Sir, you can't just start out to build something. You've got to have, or somebody has to have an idea, a plan, a diagram, a sketch. Otherwise, you'd have people building on top of each other, each in someone else's way. There'd be arguments, fights, especially over whose territory it was, whose home, whose kiva.... It would turn into a chaotic situation."

Afterwards, he had thought about the matter for half a day, and at some point, Stuart remembered saying, in a rather low tone of voice and almost to himself, "Maybe someday I'll find such a plan." That to the guffaw of Dr. Drake and the others. Overhearing Stuart's comment, an assistant quipped, "Yes, wrapped up in one of their weekly newspapers." Some students laughed as Stuart felt he wanted to hide in a sacred kiva and ask for archaeological forgiveness for challenging accepted beliefs.

Instead, he had responded with unaccustomed passion supported by personal conviction: "Listen, my grandfather was a builder of houses and apartments.

Stuart wasn't much into displays of rage. In fact, he'd seldom if ever lashed out at anyone, but at that particular instant he was compelled to lecture his superiors—something a student never did—by saying, "My grandfather never lifted a hammer without having a plan laid out before him for guidance, a plan drawn up by a bona fide architect or designer. It never entered his mind to start a house without a plan, without a drawing, without knowing where he was going. It's ludicrous to even think of doing such a thing!"

Pausing in his argument, Stuart had added, "I've read about early shipbuilders in the American Colonies. They were illiterate, but they had to have a plan to show their young workers who were just starting out. So, they took chalk and drew pictures of their ships on the timbers of the docks—that served as their plan for that particular ship." Stuart then grew quiet, his silence meeting the silence of the other archaeologists, joining the quiet of the dig, the quiet of history, and the stillness of prehistory.

Stuart belatedly reminded himself that there were some topics you just didn't discuss, certain questions left unasked. Anything having to do with the subject of Anasazi written records was one of those forbidden unopened file drawers in academia always unopened and remained locked. No one he knew had the key. That day, however, he had vowed to find the key, unlock the drawer and discover what secrets, if any, were hidden away inside.

Still, that day he had wanted to yell out with, "Behold! Here is our magnificent Pueblo Bonita, a multi-storied housing development with lots of kivas and passageways. You just can't say it began by chance and was then, willy-nilly carried out by happenstance. It couldn't have worked that way!" But as a student, Stuart had caught himself in a net of silence, wishing he had had the courage to have spoken those words out loud, wishing they would have listened to him, wishing he were in charge. Someday....

Now, this evening, standing and overlooking the surf below, Stuart silently congratulated himself, as his prayer-wish from long ago had been answered that evening in the same manner as the native shaman standing on a mountain top telling his subjects that it was summer solstice and "tomorrow you plant seeds for your new crops of corn beans and squash."

With his class's discovery—assuming they would vote to reveal it publicly in the world of academia—Stuart would receive the resultant acclaim long denied him and would be expected to look forward to unearthing fresh crops of future archaeologic discoveries. Still, flashing across his mind were two nagging questions of when would they make their public announcement, and who among them would do so? Tonight would come his students' vote. Those additional questions, if the vote was positive for the go-ahead, would need to be agreed upon. Around his living room in front of the warmth of the fireplace. Or was he once again fantasizing?

CHAPTER TWENTY-ONE

The New Mexico Dinner Menu

Inside his small 1930's Spanish Colonial style house, Stuart's staff assistant Rosalita and her twin daughters, Luna and Ynez, were preparing the dinner of enchiladas with green chile, posole, chips and salsa, plus popular New Mexican wine from where the first vineyard in the New Word had been planted to provide sacramental wine for the mission priests. Years earlier, Rosalita had introduced Stuart to real New Mexican food, and it had become his favorite cuisine.

Rosalita was from the Mexico border country. She had told him that before she was born, when it was possible to still do so, her parents had swum or waded across the Rio Bravo to where it became the Rio Grande when it was still possible to do so—at night, of course, before there were looming threats of incarceration and forced return to Mexico by the U. S. Border Patrol. The Rio Grande on the north side, the Rio Bravo on the south side. Mexico and the United States. Ever so close, ever so different, each from the other, yet each being home to bona fide human beings.

By this morning, every one of his former students had replied that they would attend the dinner. Stuart recalled their names, matched with their faces, where they were from, their enthusiasm for archaeology, and their personalities without needing to consult his field notes. Their last evening, their last campfire together was indelibly imprinted in his mind as he felt, also was on theirs.

Back at Chaco Canyon, driving the van back to campus the next day, Stuart had wondered what if some park ranger had fabricated the scroll on deerskin, dabbed some markings on it, rolled it up and inserted it in a loose space he had come across in the kiva? A joke, one good laugh for the amusement of other rangers. But pulling into campus and watching his students disembark from the van, Stuart came up short—asking himself—yes, assuring himself that the scroll was indeed a genuine Anasazi relic from antiquity!

CHAPTER TWENTY-TWO

Stuart's Students, Then and Now

No one student stood out, yet in Stuart's mind they each did. At the time of the excavation, their student faces represented a collage of ethnic enthusiasm and diversity, mixed genders, cultural and linguistic backgrounds, as well as from different geographical heritages.

The oldest student was **Barbara**, a mature mother from Albuquerque, making her return to campus to pursue her degree, after birthing and raising two children. She was always asking questions and, on many occasions, would cite her experience as a mother by questioning the role of the Anasazi mothers. "How they could have cared for their children given the only help was from each other? And, to her, the questionable advice she imagined coming from their surely-male shaman? Well, maybe they did have a female shaman, or so she reasoned out loud around an evening campfire, but she said, the male-oriented archaeological community took for granted that a shaman, of course, was male."

Barbara was focused on the essentials of the prehistory motherhood experience. She lamented the short life expectancy of Anasazi mothers, given their lack of medical care compared to what she herself had experienced, along with child birthing advice she had, and wondering what the midwife experience had been for the Anasazi mothers. Again, there were no answers from the literature that she had researched. She went on about the life that she felt must have been the birthing experience among prehistory mothers, followed by the child rearing challenges. Any different from we mothers of today? She asked, but again there were no answers from the other students, only empathy for her series of questions. What were the fathers doing to help, she wondered out loud to the other students? Maybe they did help, or maybe they didn't. What indeed were the gender roles back then in prehistory? Barbara continued her string of questions and observations, asking repeatedly. "How on earth did the Anasazi mothers keep their toddlers in tow and away from the edges of the plaza in front of their homes. "It's a sheer drop off!" she would exclaim, pointing to the houses. There are no fences, no restraints. How many children did they lose…over the edge?" She shuddered at the thought of such losses and began to cry for the mothers.

Inquisitive **Shirley** was a sociologist. At least, she told everyone that was her bent—her undergraduate major. Contrarily, so it seemed, she confided in everyone that she was interested in the aura of Anasazi ruins. She explained that she had joined the dig to study their ruins in Chaco Canyon. "It is the past," she would explain, "that is the draw for me because, coming upon them, you immediately reconstruct a view of the past, of the time when the original structure was conceived and put together. That runs the gamut from appreciation for the design, to the materials used, the labor, and the eventual purpose of the structure—that's what ruins do for me." She had added, "I'm happy to point those things out when we see our next set of ruins, to share my feelings with you."

In the course of the excavation, Shirley expanded on her point of view, especially as her love of ruins fit perfectly with Chaco Canyon. She was enjoying herself immensely having a ball, and her fellow students were soon sharing her enthusiasm.

One night around the campfire, Barbara had mothered the group by telling them, "My friends, it's not chewing peyote—although I've never done that, nor do I intend to start. No, it's gaining an insight into these ancient lives. It's having respect for their rugged existence and trying to imagine the thoughts of these Anasazi peoples. I relate them to my two kids—who have their own discoveries and visions of new ideas and coming new ways in their lives."

Following their discovery and the group's later vote to stay mum, Barbara had said, "My dear friends, we've been together on this excavation for six weeks through the heat of the day and the cold of the high desert night. We've bonded. We're seeing these Anasazi people as our friends, even as our relatives, our predecessors living here, expressing their original art on the rocks, dancing to what we perceive to be the music from their flutes. Yes, and praising their sacred idols, whoever they are and wherever they are, for they must surely have had spiritual inspiration, whether from their shaman or from their own respect for nature and the animals around them. And yes, as to our election to hold off on an announcement, with that I'm quite comfortable."

The youngest student, Stuart recalled, was **Ramon**, from Oaxaca in Mexico. His interest in the ruins and the still existing Spanish Colonial buildings of his proud city's heritage—the architectural accomplishments of his ancestors—seemed to be driving him to seek out more understanding of prehistory peoples, from whom he felt he was descendant, that is, given a genetic contribution from the Spanish Conquistadores.

Several, including Ramon and his seemingly constant buddy **Orson**, were seriously looking into developments in ground penetrating radar, which more and more was being adapted not only for oil exploration but also for locating geothermal opportunities and prehistory ruins—walls, building blocks, even the unexplained roads of the Anasazi.

Ramon was particularly curious about how the young Anasazi children began their early learning experiences. He wondered if the shaman instructed them, over and above their mothers and fathers, or if they were left on their own to discover and learn by trial and error, the school of hard knocks. He kept pressing Stuart for answers, but alas there were none, only serious speculation. It must have been this way, or that way.

Ramon commented that life expectancy was short, so there wasn't a lot of time for learning. It would have to be thorough and quick, he supposed and said so often.

Orson had disclosed to the others that he had changed careers. Previously he had wanted to be a police officer in the town of Gallup hut he had grown weary of arresting Native Americans drunk on beer and other alcoholic beverages. He confided to the others that he had come to learn that indigenous peoples had no tolerance for alcohol. Before long, Orson had decided he wanted to learn more about their culture, and so he had enrolled in Stuart's archaeology program.

One student in particular, **Victor**, stood out for his determination to pursue the new scientific technology that now made it possible to look beneath the ground's surface to locate slave quarters and to reconstruct the lives of slaves in the American South. That's where his ancestors had grown up, chained to the horrible lifestyle of slavery. Victor's desire to document and preserve as much of the slave culture as he could, write books about it, preserving the heritage of slavery, albeit bad, of course, but yet true. "As technology advances," he had said later that evening, "our field of archaeology is making great strides forward. I can feel it in my future, and years from now we'll be better at evaluating our findings here tonight, better at placing it in historical and prehistoric perspective. That's why you have my consent for our decision to wait with releasing the news to the press."

Another student was **Hans**, who was determined to advance his studies to earn a Ph. D. in archaeology and lead students on digs in the future. He was excited about what remained undiscovered in the Anasazi breadbasket of southern Colorado and northern New Mexico." After the group's vote, he had commented, "Years from now we and others in our field will better interpret them for other students coming along."

Then there was **Fletcher**, called **Stote**. He was the son of a farm family in Indiana, perhaps the least likely of all to be interested in archaeology, for there are no ruins in Indiana, few natives, and mostly stories. And it was those stories of native Americans that had intrigued Fletcher all through high school and college when he took his first anthropology course. That triggered his interest in archaeology and related disciplines.

Mary Ann saw herself pursuing a lifetime as an artist. In her sketchbook that accompanied her every place, she was continually drawing pictures of those whom she imagined to be prehistory Anasazi. In some of her sketches, she would draw her own interpretation of their rock art. She became obsessed with their gesture of a hand being held up as if to stay "stop" to those who would invade or pass by what she deemed to be warning "stop" signs on rock art.

The seventh member was **Hans**. He liked to tell people he was from a small Medieval town near Stuttgart. He was hoping for a career with one of the Max Planck Institutes specializing in the humanities. Several times he had told everyone that he felt his life's mission was to explore the development of human minds, from prehistory to the present.

When asked for his opinion about their discovery and the timing for telling people about it including it in a formal report on the excavation, Hans pondered for a while before answering, "I'm in favor of waiting before we disclose anything to our academic peers, for the following reasons: first, the material the Anasazi designer used to draw—call it either ink or charcoal has not been chemically analyzed and/or dated. For example, it may be contemporary to us, and therefore the whole artifact is not of the period. Also, the deerskin or whatever he or she drew upon for the plan has not been aged. Without either of these further investigations, we can't vouch for the plan's authenticity. And without that, we'd be accused of falsifying a find, and tarnish our reputations before we even got into the job market.

Stuart recalled applauding Hans for his perspicacious observations. The professor had then asked for other comments, which soon followed.

Barbara said she didn't want any media people calling her for an opinion or explanation, and she certainly not want any of them bothering her two children. They wouldn't know what to say and whatever they did say would add to the confusion surrounding the find.

Stote said, "Back home in Indiana, if the animals you were touting at the annual state fair were doctored with steroids, for example, you'd be disqualified, perhaps even from ever farming. No, we've got to be sure of our discovery and be certain it is authentic. Otherwise, we'll go down as forgers, and be barred from academia forever."

Mary Ann looked up from her thick sketch pad and said, "I sure don't want to be accused of drawing fake documents! Whatever I draw—and I can essentially copy what we discovered —I want it to be accurate, or perhaps an artistic interpretation, an abstraction, you might say, or possibly an artist's take of our discovery. But the underlying subject matter to be the real McCoy.

Ramon commented, "Yeah, we're not hawking tourist mementos from a roadside stand like my fellow countrymen in Mexico often do. Their look-alike copies are convincing, but not the real thing. They are selling to tourists…souvenirs, lots of them. But we here are the real thing, my friends. We are archaeologists! If we vouch for something, we better be well prepared to back up what we're saying—not that some other academics might challenge us. Let's follow legitimate accepted procedure, so we can be sure of our find and righteously defend our report. Moreover, I really want each of us to agree on how we proceed from here on out. So this is what I say to you here as we are gathered around on this beautiful campfire evening with the thrill of discovery of something momentous filling our minds."

The remining group member and the oldest in years was **Geoffrey Woodhouse**. Early on, he had asked everyone to call him **Jeff**. Though he was retired from an important career and with his own foundation which had earlier backed several archaeological digs, he insisted he was just along as one of the students on their adventure.

Outwardly, everyone seemed to get along, even with the age differences.

On a previous evening, Jeff had shared his take on thoughts about archaeology, "You know, my friends, we each study archaeology in or own way. For me, it is dipping into what we know about prehistory peoples, like our friends around here, the Anasazi. The more we study, the more field reports we read, and in some cases write the more we think we know about a culture so many eons old. But I suggest to you that we don't really have a clue about the actual lifestyle of these people. Now, here among ourselves, we learn more about each other as we ask questions of each other. Each time, we learn more about each of us. But do we really come to know each other? Will we know more about the Anasazi? Or are we fooling ourselves? I don't mean we don't try to understand one another, or try to sometimes feel like we're back living with the Anasazi. Oh, we can study each other and study the prehistory peoples, painting each of us and all of them with the colors of our own 21st century palette of colors and utilize our drawing techniques." He smiled toward Mary Ann, who nodded empathetically and smiled.

Jeff continued, "My digging buddies, no one is going to believe us if and when we ever talk about this discovery—should we do so—as momentous as it appears to be. It's a breakthrough, and no one likes breakthroughs. You know, if I were to tell my nephew who is running my foundation these days, and I'll confess he hopes to tell me I'm deranged, he'll say something like, 'Uncle Geoffrey, we just fired a researcher who argued to our board that there must surely be some sort of written language for the Anasazi and/or one of the other cultures of North America—and as you know there are dozens across the continent. No one ever wrote anything down, and that's for sure and it is common knowledge among academics in our field."

Victor spoke up, "But if you tell him you were there on the evening that we found it'?"

"No matter. He'll have me committed to Outer Archaeology where the academic nut cases convene to advance their radical ideas."

"And?" Fletcher prodded.

Jeff continued, "That's why, for now, I vote we keep this discovery under wraps, even if it does prove to be authentic someday. So, I ask you, my young friends, what good is a breakthrough if no one ever acknowledges or authenticates it? And I can tell you, as one of you pointed out, the skin, the ink, with what are the drawings—they'll all sooner or later be disallowed and tossed to the refuse pile in civilization's world of archaeological wonders. They'll be right down there with the 15th Century Chinese junk supposedly buried in the mud of the Sacramento River somewhere in the Carquinez Straight east of San Francisco, or with the stone houses of New England that purportedly date back to the Norsemen of 1,000 or so years ago." He added with a derisive snort, "Just think about the forgery of the Piltdown Man!"

Stuart recalled, lacking the proper words to dispute Jeff's pessimism. So he told his students, "Jeff's foundation represents a respected tradition in archaeological discoveries around the world. If they won't vouch for us, then...well, then I suspect that may make the decision for us."

Slowly, all the heads nodded.

After a short break, the vote was taken, fair and square, and the decision reached: "Mum's the word for now until we meet again as a group—sooner or later, but sooner, I hope." Stuart wondered if anything would change in their minds or in the annals of archaeology in the intervening time when they were to meet again.

So, they took their vote and agreed—it was to be on Stuart's call, a year or so later.

CHAPTER TWENTY-THREE

That Vote Had Followed Further Discussion

It is tough in academia to simply leave a topic on the floor like spilled milk for somebody else to mop up. It seems there is someone who always wants to re-visit the last topic and jawbone it to its absurd limits. But this group of students wasn't that way. The following morning back in class, however, they did decide, with Stuart's support, to briefly review their decision to wait to announce their discovery, or conversely, to stay mum.

Barbara spoke first. "Friends, I want to know just how these ancient people did build Pueblo Bonita without squabbling with each other over whose house was under construction, where each of the kivas were to be dug and who was to be admitted into each, plus how were they were to decide the layout of the passages that snake through the complex. Yes, in my view, somebody or some committee had to be in charge."

Ramon interrupted, "Yes, there had to be a plan, either drawn on deerskin, like I think we just found, or else with a plan in his or her head and expressed on the scroll we found."

Stote said, "And everyone living there would have agreed upon it ahead of time. I mean in advance of actual construction, like farm fields in Indiana. Back home, we just don't start in with our plows, each farmer, elbowing other farmers away, then starting to seed a field with whatever seed we have leftover in the barn from last season—that would lead to tractor wars and chaos and clearly not be the type farming from a plan advanced to us from the County Agent and the Department of Agriculture back in Washington. I think that would have been the case here—no plan, no action."

Mary Ann said, "But without a written language, without even an agreed-upon spoken language, how would they have communicated with each other, either with or without a plan?"

Stuart suggested, "Maybe they had a language that everyone spoke, and everyone understood."

Victor answered, "But without a dictionary, how would you know what word to use?"

Barbara commented, "Dictionaries are relatively new things—thanks to Mr. Webster. I mean, we didn't always have dictionaries. You know, think about Chaucer and his spellings. But then, at least, folks in England had a written language...of sorts, I mean."

"But," Ramon, said, "You know. There's more to language than a trained typewriter."

"Go on," Stuart remembered urging.

"Well, it's simple," Frank said.

"No, it's not," Victor argued.

Indignantly Stote declared, "Ever watch the birds, farm animals, like I have done? They'll communicate with each other, either while flying or grazing or galloping. Sounds, such as grunts, physical movement of their tales, their heads bobbing, their noses rooting and snorting."

Mary Ann added, "And there's whistling. Back home my friends are good at whistling...tunes, for sure, but warnings, expressions of pleasure, you know, your feelings, emotions, even boys cat calling at the girls."

Geoffrey said, "Yes, last time I traveled to Spain, I really noticed the non-verbal expressions, such as sucking in air or out. Each breath, so to speak, had a different meaning. I came to realize that, but I never felt I quite got it all straight, so I never tried to emulate any of those air movement sounds."

Victor offered, "Musicians make their own sounds, with their instruments. Drummers can get very emotional on how hard and fast they strike with their sticks."

Ramon asked, "So, how did our Anasazi find here," and he gestured at their scroll, "communicate some sort of advanced design or layout for Pueblo Bonita?"

Mary Ann answered, "Obviously with what we found in this niche in the kiva wall—the deerskin, or whatever it is."

"Yes," Barbara said, "The markings…they mean something, don't you think?"

Geoffrey nodded and pointed to the markings, "This would be where each house is to go, where each kiva is to be dug, where each passageway is to run, but there must be some sort of indication as to whose house is whose."

Having listened carefully to everyone, Stuart concluded, "Okay, then we'll meet in Big Sur at my house in due course and take our vote. Meanwhile, I'll swear my campus chemist to secrecy and ask her to take a sample of what I will call 'ink' for her laboratory age test."

* * *

Later Stuart comforted himself with retrospective wisdom, He thought about his career and acknowledged that he had never made the headlines like one of those sponsored digs in the jungles of Central America or in the even more academically popular sands of Egypt. He lamented that those headline locations for excavations were the ones that received ample funding from the well-endowed academic institutions and their supporting non-profit think tanks and charitable foundations. Their financial support of an excavation was followed by colorful stories in such popular magazines like National Geographic, along with internet web stories that extolled the lead archaeologist's skills. Stuart somewhat forlornly reflected that during his years of study at the University of Kansas and later at Arizona State, he had chosen the remote Southwest for it offered him the exploration of the pre-history culture in which he had become most intrigued during his studies—the Anasazi, "they who are not us," according to the Navajo interpretation and translation of the word

Thinking more about the vote of his students and himself that night at the edge of their excavation, Stuart wondered as to the wisdom of their action, and of course his, as well, for he could have vetoed their decision, telling his student that keeping a find secret was not authorized in academia. Moreover, his reputation was on the line, and he was subject to having his name dragged through the dirty mud of disgraced academia. He felt certain that, with their knowing the extent of his personal career risks, they would have each backed away from their seminal vote.

So, why did he allow his students to proceed with the vote? Why didn't he stop them? What was he to gain from doing it? What were they to gain? And then they were presumably coming to his house to once again perhaps support their continuing consensus to postpone any announcement, at least for the time being, but what was "the time being?" And how did he know they would so vote? He didn't. That made him uncertain about his own feelings.

He was sure, if he were to counter their new vote, they would, as his former students, go along with his change of heart by deciding to make the news public. Or would they? Each and every one of them? Wouldn't they have to have a unanimous vote? He wasn't sure that restrictive condition was a provision of their campfire vote that evening, though they did all agree. Yes, it was unanimous. Nevertheless, any changed decision would be attributed to him, for he was their professor, their leader, the authority setting the ethical example for his former class of devoted students.

Stuart reviewed his two choices—first to go along with his students, if that was to be their choice this evening. Yet, he was well aware such a decision, if ever and whenever found out and publicized, would risk him being accused by contemporaries in academia of withholding a vital new discovery for years. Or secondly, receiving ridicule from his contemporaries for forging or else revealing a highly improbable piece of evidence about the Anasazi, their structures, even their ability to communicate to one another. Either way it was a No-Win situation for him, a loss no matter which way he chose. And his students had no idea of the depth of his dilemma. Surely, he must try to tell them, or else remain silent. The silence of obscurity. That wouldn't be proper...no, sir...no way!

When his students had signed up for his class, he assumed they all knew that Pueblo Bonita was an internationally registered archaeological site, as well as a recognized tourist attraction on the national register of historic places. It was on the state list as well, up there with the pyramids, New Grange in Ireland, and Stonehenge in England. He could go on an on—although let's face it, among ruins, there is a limit, a finality, an accepted list, a hall of fame, a treasure roll for antiquity. Pueblo Bonita was a part of it—a ruin for all time, for eternity, for ever and ever.

It suddenly struck Stuart that none of those other world-famous sites had any sort of building plan—they were each in the same undocumented situation as all of Chaco Canyon, and thus so was Pueblo Bonita, in the center of Chaco Canyon. No one, at least as far as he knew or as far as the literature had revealed had found a plan, drawn on deerskin or some other skin showing what went where. If he were to announce that Pueblo Bonita was to become the exception, right off, he would not be believed. He would become the laughing stock of archaeology, for sure. His academic career would become dust bin material, added to the middens of broken pottery that always existed at the outskirts of an ancient Anasazi community.

CHAPTER TWENTY-FOUR

The Day of the Student Dinner

Stuart made a dash into Rosalita's kitchen to help himself to the blue corn chips and organic salsa. The combo always gave his mind a jolt, a prod to explore new ideas.

Back outside, engulfed by another incoming Rorschach test-like formation of billowing evening coastal fog, Stuart reviewed the question of who it was among the Anasazi who had drawn this scroll— the presumed plan for Pueblo Bonita? Was it the shaman? Was it a person or persons with direction from the shaman? He wondered if the Anasazi ever endowed someone with such an assignment? Some of them did specialize in firing clay pots, some the granary ceramic storage pots, some ground the corn, some engaged in the hunt. Were those tasks gender specific? A recent find, he reminded himself, questioned the traditionally-thought gender roles, but that was just one study. It went against the common knowledge, but then who wrote the common knowledge? How many times in history had the common knowledge been uprooted, discarded, then rewritten? And then, later on, once again challenged?

Like a flash from a lighthouse beacon, the whole story played across Stuart's mind. Adrift in the fog bank of his career and his knowledge of the story of Chaco Canon played like the frames of. movie one after the other, full of native prehistory people in their presumably customary attire. Stuart was full of insights into the ancient culture. He was part of it. He was there. He was one of them. He was back there with them. Their story was unfolding: Prehistory unfurled before him, but then....

* * *

The Shaman...with Answers?

Billows of the evening fog from off the Pacific were rapidly consuming Stuart. Staring into the overhead fog, Stuart felt himself being transported into a different scene. In this amorphous state, Stuart was consumed by the abstraction of another time and place, a far-distant yet not an entirely unfamiliar scene.

Inconspicuously, once again Stuart was moving amidst a gathering of ancient Anasazi folks, dressed as they were in their period attire. As previously, his own blue eyes and whiter skin stood out, quite obviously revealing him as not being one of them. He had no painted face markings, no wild hat. As a distraction, he had a sudden urge to talk to the little children, many naked, who were now looking up at him, curiosity written across their young faces. He smiled at a little boy who laughed in return, the exchange of merriment bolstering Stuart's spirits.

Looking at the crowd, Stuart asked himself where was the shaman, his presumed friend from his previous visitation episode? The native leader was nowhere, and obviously no help in making him feel comfortable among the natives.

Stuart realized he must return to reality. He reluctantly conceded he didn't really know anything, or what to believe. After all, he had taught his students, and conversed with them, answering their questions, thriving in their curiosity with explanations about these

116

prehistory people. Stuart stood steady, alone in an antique world of time.

Stuart lamented, where were his students now? Oh, yes, they were all coming—later this evening. But why hadn't any of them come with him to this Anasazi village. Why weren't they here to simply lend the strength of their numbers to his presence? And what about his cell phone? Could he get a signal here? What a stupid question. Maybe, if he were to just show the shaman his cell phone and offer to make a call for him, he could begin to bond with the holy man. Although, in his life, he had had little success in bonding with any of today's holy men and women. But was the shaman really a holy man? And what was the god or were the gods they worshipped, or was their god the shaman himself? In his life, Stuart had concluded that some head persons thought of themselves as gods to whom their congregation must pray, demonstrating their unlimited respect. He reached for his cell phone, but then realized it was still in Rosalita's kitchen where he had set it down to fill his grasp with blue corn chips and salsa.

Stuart tried to recall his conversations with students, especially around their campfire on the edge of their dig. Often students come up with gems, but Stuart was unable to remember any words of student wisdom at this moment.

Then he detected a different beat to the Anasazi singing. The men were chanting while some of the women were playing a tune on their primitive flutes. Well, it wasn't primitive to them, it was on their hit parade list of acceptable tunes, as up to date as were all the prehistory folks in this crowd. What were they signing, and what was the melody of the tune? It was all new, all strange. The shaman was now in the middle of the singers and the flute players were encouraging everyone on.

Stuart almost felt—yes, he did feel the magical beat of the music. He began to move in rhythm with the primitive notes as they sounded. The shaman saw him and, in relief to Stuart, nodded his approval. Some of the women were bare chested, and beautiful in their own prehistory way, not smiling.

Roads, Stuart thought. Yes, these are the roads leading in all directions out from Chaco Canyon. These are the roads discovered by Charles Lindberg in the 1930s while flying over New Mexico in an experiment of pioneering aerial photography. The roads surprisingly showed up, not on the ground, but to the surprise of the locals, rather on the photographs. Plus, Stuart ruminated, the Anasazi didn't have the wheel. What is their mission? What is in their minds? But where were these roads leading? And from where would the natives come? And where would they go? And why? And when? And how often? And carrying what? And did they have some sort of carts with wheels? And did their dogs pull the carts? The Anasazi had pet dogs. Off in the distance he saw some of their dogs playing, as little children ran with them.

Continuing to observe and ponder what he was watching, either actually or in his imagination, Stuart recalled some of the fantasies he had envisioned years ago during his many excavations in New Mexico, Arizona and even Colorado as he had studied the ancient Anasazi. These vivid scenarios now ran across his mind like endless repeating frames of colorful movie clips.

And then with excitement, Stuart heard a car horn, then another.

CHAPTER TWENTY-FIVE

Horns Blowing, Horns Announcing the Students
and Danica's Arrival

The scene suddenly changed and abruptly returned to the reality of the present. Automobile horns were announcing the news of his student arrivals. Yes, here they were coming—at last to his house overlooking the Pacific Ocean.

Looking beyond the first cars, Stuart spotted Danica. Seeing him, she smiled and in unison, they each waved as she came toward Stuart. She stopped to introduce herself to several of his students getting out of their cars. Stuart called out to her an Italian welcome and then almost in the same breath began to greet his own students, one after the other. Finally, there followed a long awaited and overdue embrace from Danica who whispered "So, this place on the edge of the ocean where you live, Stuart Sweet, my favorite Ph. D?"

With a smile, Stuart nodded, adding, "I should tell you that Kip and Dorothy Overman are also flying in this evening. When I told them what is going on with our voting and the debate we're going to undertake after our dinner, they immediately wanted to be part of our discussion so that they can convey the evening's narrative to the Max Planck folks back in Berlin."

Danica responded, "I don't know about that. I want to discuss it with you. "Anyway, it'll be good to see them again. We need to bring them up to date on the Conference…and," she added," the aftermath. Not easy to do…under the circumstances, but necessary and in our own words. They've always been very supportive."

Danica asked members of the group now being assembled in Stuart's living room, "What is to be the outcome of our discussions here tonight?" To Stuart, she commented, "You mentioned in your letter that you thought none of us—you and I and your students wanted—and I'm guessing here--to be relegated to the outback archives of archaeology."

Stuart spoke to everyone in the room, "That's up to all of us this evening in our vote after our Southwest dinner."

Victor didn't hesitate to add, "I'm ready to decide."

Stote said, "Yeah, let's get on with the dinner and discussion."

Privately Stuart asked Danica, "And what news of Bernie?"

"Happily, she replied, "He's been freed of any charge. Moreover, he's decided to pursue his Ph. d. degree, so, he's back in classes. He asked me about putting his name on our paper about the Etruscans. "He's flying in tonight, and should be here any minute."

"What'd you tell him?"

"I'd talk to you, but I hinted that as far as the Etruscans are concerned, the three of us compose our own paper and, because he doesn't know the Anasazi, he'll withhold his name to whatever you and your students write." That is, if they so decide to publish. So, it's a reciprocal deal, as they say.

Stuart reflected on the gravity of the task ahead for the group this evening. Turning toward them, he quickly got their attention and said, "Before we go into dinner, I want to say this to you all, Academia has its rules of performing the research, its rules of reporting research, rigid, fixed. It would take a lot of opinions to budge them, and that means a lot of evidence, and a lot of ideas based on findings. Can we dare question things here tonight? Things that have been established for semesters, for school years, for dates going back how far? Yes, decades. And do it tonight? Well, we had better get with it." He wondered where were Kip and Dorothy? their plane should have landed by now, and they should be here.

In uncertainty, Stuart wavered. Suddenly he was thinking of things from the shaman's point of view. Assuming he would understand the words the shaman was saying, he believed he was likely saying, "So much for new ideas. We don't need them. We don't want them. We're just fine the way we are…here tonight and every night."

To himself, Stuart acknowledged that these Anasazi locals had no writing, no symbols, no formal way of even communicating a new idea to each other, to consider it or then adopt it…no book of rules, no written code of conduct, no constitution, and to speak. No way of acceptance of even one new idea. Kill change. Therefore, kill new ideas. For one thing, if someone floated a new idea, the shaman would probably not want to adopt it for fear of losing his coveted position of authority. Stuart added to his thoughts while smiling, "That may be the way the vote goes here on the shores of the Pacific when we have concluded our evening together."

Regardless of the discipline directing the academic field of archaeology, there always seemed to be competitors, either in the immediate faculty or in the world of academia land who were ready and able to critique his field notes, his finds, and the ideas he came to advance from his new discoveries.

Stuart could recall experiences, even before he earned his Ph.D. degree, where he encountered jealous critiques from his review board, and from those who felt his formal education was inadequate. Well, maybe he was misguided, for his dissertation was almost trashed from his voiced rebuttal to the criticism, yet he stood steadfastly by his thesis, claiming its premise that there was creativity among prehistory people, who often had their ingenuity put down by local leaders for feared losing their control over the community. What with their power, they continued to dominate by instilling fear and, on the other hand, awe, over their fellow men and women students attending big state universities. That was accepted policy in archaeology, he had feared at the time, and he had been frightened for advocating otherwise. Eventually, however, after a close vote his thesis was accepted and he did receive his degree and could now be addressed as Doctor Sweet. He had proudly added "Dr." to his name on his busines card and in the list of department faculty. He could sing articles that way, and even work on his book publication, summarizing his findings of life among the lives of the prehistory Anasazi in the Four Corners area. For that he was proud.

And now he had backed himself into a corner where everything he had worked for and justifiably earned could all go down the drain of discarded archaeological thought.

* * *

Nevertheless, Stuart led everyone into the kitchen for introductions to Rosalita and her twin daughters. Ynez and Luna passed out plates, cutlery and napkins to each guest and served them bowls of posole with enchiladas covered with Hatch green chili salsa from New Mexico.

They all found chairs in the living room, which was warmed by the fire in the kiva fireplace. Soon afterwards Bernard Monterossa passed through the kitchen, followed by Dorothy and Kip Overman. Each joined the group in the living room. Stuart gave them firm handshakes plus there were tender hugs from Danica, followed by introductions all around, while glasses of New Mexico wine were available.

CHAPTER TWENTY-SIX

Aftermath of the Dinner Meal
Decisions

Finalizing explanatory discussions about the regional food, Stuart posed a question to his many guests, "What is it about these pre-history people of ours who have come to dominate our adult lives as educated archaeologists? I refer to those of us here this evening—representing the Etruscans and the Anasazi.

"We all know that many cultures, groups of people around the world pre-date events like the Industrial Revolution, written language, coded books of law, organized religions that have impacted our lives. So, what is about the folks who have gone before that calls us to study them? Why do we dig, excavate, research, and write our papers? There are many more peoples around the world—people who pre-date events impacting our lives, such as the Industrial Revolution, adaption of the written language, adhering to the coded books of law, following the canons of organized religions, in other words...us...who live here today. What is it about these folks who have gone before? Why do we study them? Why do we dig, excavate, research and write our papers? We can't talk to them. We can't ask them questions to access their lives, beliefs, values, and wisdom."

Stuart paused. Some sipped wine. Some waited, anticipation leading their thoughts as he said, "I want to suggest the beginnings of an answer that I anticipate will start off our discussion here this evening."

He then began the introduction to their evening assignment, "My friends, allow me to go back in time to the 16th Century. The French who had set sail to the New World began to explore the native tribes in what was to become French Canada. To their amazement and curiosity, these Europeans discovered native peoples who spoke a different language, wore different clothes, and had different customs. The people lived in accommodations the French didn't recognize or relate to – certainly different from those found in traditional cities in far-away France. So, what did the French do to take advantage of this learning opportunity and enhance their knowledge of the native pre-history people?" Stuart waited and then said, "The French studied the native language of the New World inhabitants. They learned to speak it and to communicate with the natives. At the same time, a number of the natives chosen because they seemed highly intelligent, were transported to France to study French society.

"Soon the natives could speak French and the French could converse with the natives, and each could ask each the other questions about their lifestyles, customs, language, and beliefs."

Stuart asked his guests, "Do we do this today, 300 and 400 years later? No, we think that today native peoples should adopt our ways, our dress, our language, our religion." He looked round the room. "So, where does that leave us with the Etruscans and the Anasazi, as far as learning from them, benefiting them in their identities and life experience, as well as improving our own lot as we learn from past civilizations? In other words, are we learning from those who have gone before?"

"I've never heard that about the French in Canada," Dorothy Overman commented.

Addressing Stuart's query, Bernard said, "There's so much we can learn from the ancients—things we may be uncomfortable or un-familiar with and maybe even unwilling to accept. That's because it goes against what we have learned, studied, and believed to be what took place among the ancient people who have preceded us."

Dania said, smiling at Bernard, "Like the Etruscans calling out to the later-in-time American Revolutionaries and inspiring a name for the Thirteen American Colonies."

Bernie added, "We can thank that 18th Century ocean-going merchant from Philadelphia who explored the Etruscan heritage in the area of Tuscany."

Dorothy Overman reacted, "Well, that's a nice story, but in to-day's world it is not a guiding light for we archaeologists."

"How so?" asked Victor.

Kip filled in for his wife, "In today's real world of funding explo-rations, excavations and research, costs are enormous. Gone are the days of the rich amateur archaeologists embarking on his (or her) exciting little adventure. No, it is big business, big budgets, and—here's the rub—big grants from big institutions. For example, how many grants have been added to study the Etruscans? I'll tell you the simple answer—zero, that is— unless you can somehow link your exploration grant to the Romans, and ideally to a male Roman em-peror." Kip went on, "Well, that's where the Max Planck Institute can influence the flow of money and focus the interest of universities and institutions."

Dorothy added, "…Yes, and we thank them, but we're taking here about the future, and for research by younger students as they come out of the real academic world of the 21st century."

Stuart held up his hand to say, "My friends, fortunately we have this evening to make a determination, in our own way, deciding here tonight whether to address what we have discovered about the past, through the eyes of the Etruscans and the minds of the Anasazi, to add to the story of past years and, even more importantly, to influence the future thoughts of our profession. What we have been trained to do, we are good at, and now we will be even better at or 50 years from now, I mean such will be the future for young students entering the field today."

While there had been many other excavations throughout his undergraduate and then graduate program, many cited in his dissertation, Stuart found the whole experience with this particular seminar of these nine students coming back to him in a king tide of memories. Fondly Stuart relished those evening back and forth conversations as they had gathered around the campfire. There, looking up into the fading cobalt blue sky of their day, peering out into the endless nothingness of dusk and space, Stuart had marveled at the purity of the New Mexico sky--the most deep blue he had ever seen, hiding in its luster the secrets of the unknown of an endless universe, as endless, he had remarked to his students as the questions raised by studying the prehistory Anasazi people who had ever so many years ago inhabited that part of the American Southwest.

Yet, from recent research into its illusive story, which was somewhat better known today in the days since his dig and his talks with the students, Stuart smiled as he thought of the eager faces and sharp minds of these students. Some were planning to go on to explore and add to the scientific database of theories and knowledge of what lay in the lands below those intriguing blue skies. It was much like how his career had tried to explore the hidden lives and culture of the prehistory people who had lived in the American Southwest as long ago as two thousand years.

Coming back to the present moment, Stuart again took charge and addressed Danica, "Will you please set an agenda for us this evening?"

As Danica nodded, Kip Overman offered, "Parenthetically I

must say, and briefly, I know from personal experiences, supported by many in the field, that when you perceive a research project
in Northern Mexico relating to the Anasazi, the institutional grant
people lose interest very quickly when they realize your project was
not related to the Aztecs or the Olmecs but to—and what where their
names—the peoples living just south of the border in far-northern
Mexico."

Danica said, "Okay, we have two topics to discuss and two decisions to make here this evening. First, we have to decide about the
existence of the Anasazi scroll and whether or not to go public with
the news of it. Secondly, we're going to let Bernard lead the debate
about the Etruscans and the 13 American Colonies."

Stuart asked Danica, "Is that our agenda?"

She replied, "Does everyone agree to that plan—at least the ma-
jority—here this evening?"

There was no dissent.

Stuart then proposed, "Mary Ann, will you please go first with
your decision?"

Mary Ann, clutching her notebook and turning to a drawing she
had made of the scroll found in the kiva, began, "Okay, I say we go
public with this discovery. It has shed a new light on the capabilities
of our Anasazi, improving the public image of their skills at building.
After all, Pueblo Bonita was the largest residential building in North
America until just recently in modern time. It was multi-story, as
were other buildings in the 18 pueblos of New Mexico and Arizona."

* * *

To himself, Stuart recalled that he and his students had discussed
how the ancestors of the Anasazi had walked from Siberia across
the Bering land bridge during those long-ago eras when the ice had

melted. How far they had walked, sometime along the shoreline of what became Alaska. Going inland, they had then walked and walked to what would eventually become—unbeknownst to the migrants—the touching of the Four Corners of Arizona, New Mexico, Utah and Colorado. All in due course, Stuart recalled. today and in the future, such an absurd trek would be important only if the migrants had left a village that might become a tourist attraction for folks wanting an eco-tourist experience, or those on a cruise ship docking nearby and seeking a shore-time excursion to sell at extra cost to passengers."

Stuart reminded himself of the many deep questions he had asked himself and his students, as they had met on the many mornings at the site of their excavation: What were those human beings thinking as they walked, day after day, month after month across such new and unfamiliar lands? Were they thinking at all, or just following some leader urging them onward? But why? Were they, for some reason, emotion, simply moving on, one foot in front of the other, regardless of the rain, the snow, icy cold, the boiling hot sun....?

Mary Ann spoke up, adding to her previous comments, "I suggest that the occasional restoration effort in Pompeii and Herculaneum showed the merits of restoration for tourists. "To the extent we can get people interested, as tourists, in the past. I say, yes, get folks everywhere interested in those who have gone before."

Stuart silently reflected on the morning when the women students wanted to discuss the arduous days of young mothers with their children, as they persevered on this endless trek across a nothing place. Shirley asked, "How did the leader of the group inspire the others to continue on this long walk? What did he, or she, tell them about where they were going?"

Stote had asked one day, "When they stopped, how long did they camp, and did they build shelters? Stuart recalled telling them that since the migration, the sea had risen so much that if had the mi-grants had built structures for temporary shelter—had they halted for days or even years, today the seas would have risen so much that their efforts, their remaining ruins, their landmarks, would by now be obscured. That led to even more questions. Barbara opined that a leader who could continue to inspire under such unknown cir-cumstance of harsh weather and hostile animals, must have exuded charisma, for in her own student life she had not followed anyone. Then she had laughed, adding, "Under such dire circumstances... who would do so?"

Stuart had asked the students how the leader for their march across Alaska had been chosen?

"I know," Shirley the sociologist declared, waving her hands in the air for emphasis. She said that the leader was the disinherited son of a tribal chief and, in a rage, the son had gone off on his own recruiting followers with stories of riches and maybe better game if they would all follow him into a new territory in the eastern direc-tion, to which he had pointed."

Victor said, "No, I think there was disagreement about which god to worship. Shirley suggested one of the immigrants had had a vision about a new goddess and that this goddess lived in the east where the sun came up, and if they were to go to the destination, they could meet this goddess and receive her blessings and be happy ever after."

"And what if someone, in a rage of discontent, rose up, and slew the leader, and assumed the leadership role himself or herself?"

"Suggesting they turn back?"

"Or choose a different direction...."

"Or build huts and settle down there and hunt the game and raise their families...."

Those remarks led to heated debates among Stuart's guests about the qualities and techniques of leadership. Several asked, "Were those qualities any different in those prehistoric times than today?" From there on, Stuart recalled, the discussions ensued, then continued around the evening campfire and into the next morning.

Several of the students continued to talk about baby care and the trials of raising babies while trekking across a no man's land, and even of giving birth in such a wilderness in such primitive circumstances. Several agreed with Stuart, life expectancy back then must have been, and indeed was short. He recalled suggesting that in today's world, the fact that we have much longer life expectancies, means we should expect more of ourselves than just completing a long walk to nowhere to contribute more to society. Mary Ann shared that that was why she was in college and why she wanted to know more about the motivations of prehistory peoples "everywhere. But here is where I want to sketch them."

Stuart told himself, once again, that thought has been with the species since its inception, depending on what date in time you assigned its beginnings. Thought was human. Imagination was human. Creativity was human. And he and his students were each human. Yet, the Anasazi are not like us today, and we are not like them. Although…. yes, his field notes, his moonlit night under the stars, being cold in the high desert, searching in the center of a remote area, but one that had one been home to a prehistory civilization. What were those people thinking? What were their leaders thinking? What abstractions did they believe?

They knew, or had learned enough about the summer and winter solstices to construct a calendar so that they could and would plant their seeds of corn, beans, and squash, and would grow their crops, harvest them and eat them. They knew enough to collect rainwater in ponds and the run-off from high places so they could water their crops between the infrequent rain storms.

But what did they think about the world? Stuart had asked his students for their insights. Sitting along with them above the Grand Kiva in Chaco Canyon. he had wanted to ask the people down below in the kiva, about their dances, while they arranged their songs, again, and then asked himself for what seemed like thousands of times. He told his students to converse with the peoples during their ceremony in the Grand Kiva. He directed them to listen to the drums, and the singing, plus the magical music on their flutes. If only, he suggested, we could just transcribe, translate the vibes from the people into a paragraph followed by another paragraph of interpretation from himself and from the students. After all, he was supposed to have thoughts, too—conclusions, summaries, onto which they might each apply their own intelligence, their own learning, their own re-search to devise what life among these prehistory people was like if you were back there in time as a participant in their culture.

Thinking back about the experience overlooking the ceremony of the prehistory folks gathered in the Grand Kiva, Stuart recalled his students watching as he urged them to imagine and insert them-selves into the scene. He concluded his students must have thought him quite nutty, but then, he consoled himself, his mission, as their teacher, was to encourage them to think, to imagine, to venture be-yond the text book language. Wasn't that his vote? Yes, but in his own teaching efforts, sometimes he only evoked only unwanted retorts from his students. For example, he smiled as he recalled one young woman accused him of sexual bias when he suggested the men were thinking about construction methods for new home blocks while the women were focused on their babies and their growing children. "The women had wider interests," the student suggested. And when he asked her to explain, she showed hostility, suggesting that even in prehistory times, women were being discriminated against.

He had attempted to broaden the discussion, directing they

would go around one by one, offering their opinions as to what might be on the minds of the Anasazi peoples as they sang and danced and played their little crafted flutes in the Grand Kiva down below their vantage point. "Imagine them, one by one... see them there...get into their minds please," he implored. "Even though it has been a thousand plus years, our archaeological exercise this evening is to imagine. We need to exercise our thinking muscles and to imagine... imagine....and put this concept on paper."

* * *

By now It was present time and the fog outside was thick.

The elder Jeff said, "Here's what we're going to do tonight. He then dipped into his knowledge of California history and told them, "There used to be a train that ran along these cliffs, bringing passengers from San Francisco to Big Sur. But, after so many landslides from winter rains cutting service, and so many repairs of the line, they gave up trying to rebuild it. You can still see some of the tunnels in cliffsides, though." He added, "You know, it's much like our mission here this evening."

"How so," asked Stote.

"Well," Jeff began, "ours is a task without guidance as to the correct route ahead. Thee are many hurdles blocking our way to a successful path forward."

CHAPTER TWENTY-SEVEN

Student and Faculty Decisions

Barbara was elected to go first. Ramon had commented, "Anyone who has raised two young boys has got to have good judgment and be the most mature and wise of all of us, so I suggest she go first."

Producing a yellow tablet, Stuart signaled he was prepared to take notes and began by entering Barbara's name.

Barbara began, "I believe the decision must rest with Dr. Sweet. He is the most experienced of all of us, knows the academic system better and has most at stake here. Further, he will know how to arrange to date the deerskin and the ink or whatever it is that has been imposed on the scroll to form the plan or whatever it is that we discovered that night a year ago."

Victor gathered his thoughts and began, "It's sort of like the slave quarters in the Old South. Best if we could talk to the slaves and get their take on what life was like, but of course we're not able to find a slave—their descendants, of course, but they didn't live the life of a slave. Similarly, we can't locate an Anasazi person and ask them who drew the plan, if that's what it is, for there are no Anasazi alive today and their descendants, who I have read about, have denied an intimate knowledge of life a thousand years ago.

Accordingly, I think it is up to Dr. Sweet what we do with our find—up to his judgment, for he is the most knowledgeable of all of us.'

Stote went next, saying, "The way to learn about farming is to ask a farmer. The same is true here in my opinion. We need to ask an Anasazi. But there are none around, so the next best is Dr. Sweet himself, as he knows them, understands them, at least better than I do or I suspect any of the rest of us. But because of the time difference between us and them –the ancient Anasazi—I'm reluctant to bare their secrets, to release the deerskin to examination by experts. I don't think there are experts. If you want to know about farming, ask a farmer. I you want to know the life of an Anasazi, ask an Anasazi, not some academic who may not know any more than any of us. So, I vote to keep our find a secret or to trust its possible disclosure to Dr. Sweet."

Mary Ann stood up, unfurled her sketch book, and said, "I've sketched the markings on our deerskin, but I don't know what they mean, and I'd have to ask an Anasazi for that information. I'm content to draw and to interpret, but not to disclose something that I do not have confirmation of—that is, its age, its authenticity, for all I know it may be a hoax—albeit a fun and exciting hoax if that is indeed what it is, and I don't know, so I vote to defer to Dr. Sweet, to his judgment, to his knowledge in university life."

Hans was next. He said, "I'm a believer in the scientific method, and we've learned the scientific lessons about archaeology from Dr. Sweet here, so I think he is the one to decide. I'm trying to follow the mindset of Max Planck over a hundred years ago who was one of the most brilliant minds of Germany and Europe back then, along with Einstein. Their minds were open and inquisitive, as are ours, yet Dr. Sweet is the one in charge of the dig and the one to decide the path to follow, if there is one, ahead."

Orson said, "In police work, there is a right and a wrong. Sometimes the very rules of the home base must be rearranged areas in law and in society. I really don't know what path to say we follow, and I fear that, by chance our scroll may be some sort of a forgery, a hoax prepared. Then we'll all look silly, especially our professor." He looked at Stuart and said, "Dr. Sweet, so, I'm in favor of keeping the whole discovery under wraps. Yet someday—soon or far off—someone else will discover a similar artifact, as only a small percentage of these Anasazi sites have been excavated, and just maybe someone will find a similar scroll, and then we can say, "Oh, yeah, we found one, too, years ago. Here it is.""

Jeff spoke up next, "I've been troubling over this for some time, and I agree with most of you. Dr. Sweet is the authority here, and so I believe it his decision to make it public, and if so, now, or to not do so at all."

Ramon went last and said, "My architectural accomplishments in Old Mexico are pubic and are photographed and studied, as most of them are preserved, the ones that are in ruins are still studied. We learn from ruins and we learn more from the more we study. To withdraw this scroll from the pubic record is to deny other students of prehistory peoples the opportunity to add to their knowledge base. I think we have to disclose the findings and add it to the body of knowledge about the Anasazi."

Stuart said, "We'll ask each of you for your vote, one by one, as to your decision: keep our find a secret or to go to press with our discovery. And that will be that.

They all voted "yes, reveal our discovery." The kiva insert scroll with the presumed plan for Pueblo Bonita would be disclosed by Stuart through the university publicity department.

Stuart turned to Danica, winking at Bernard, and said, "Now it's your turn."

Danica looked at Bernard and asked, "How do you want to go forward with your information?"

Bernard said, I'm in favor of telling it through the paper that you and I and Stuart write, giving due credit to your late husband Jackson and his sacrifice."

Looking at Kip and Dorothy Overman and receiving their visual consents, Danica said, "And so be it." She added, "We have achieved what the Max Planck Institute set out to accomplish several years ago—providing excitement and enthusiasm for students in archaeological programs worldwide, as well as expanding the interest among people everywhere. I know Jackson will be pleased that we have set new ideas for archaeology."

Stuart hugged Danica and said, "The existence of a deer skin will be disclosed, and the world will take another look at the American Revolution and the reasons for it."

THE END

AUTHOR'S FURTHER DEDICATION

For Helen

WHO IS JON FOYT?

And how can he have written this archaeological novel?

Yes, he's an old white man from Indianapolis, but with plenty of experiences in his 90-plus years, plus a runaway imagination fed by hyperphantasia.

He attended Shortridge High School, as did Kurt Vonnegut, Dan Wakefield, and Senator Richard Lugar.

He's lived in most parts of the U.S., including California's Great Central Valley.

He's built homes, worked in banking, electronics, and managed radio broadcasting stations in Oregon and Idaho.

He's studied Buddhism, and been a Presbyterian.

He was a tour leader for Crow Canyon Archaeological Center in Cortez, Colorado.

He's served in the Armor Corps of the U.S. Army and in Military Intelligence during the Korean War.

He has a degree in Journalism from Stanford University plus an MBA from there.

He later attended the University of Georgia to study Historic Preservation and the Confederacy.

He's experienced a host of medical problems plus the passing of his wife Lois with whom he collaborated in writing their earlier novels.

He has lived in two retirement communities before moving to Rossmoor where he has served as president of the Stanford Club and written for the weekly Rossmoor News.

He has completed 60 full length marathons and innumerable shorter races.

NOTABLE ADULT NOVELS
BY JON FOYT

Last Train From Mendrisio (with Lois—offshore Trusts)

Time to Retire – Life in a Retirement Community

Marcel Proust in Taos – A Cat Retires in Taos

The Third Half of Our Lives – Two Old Guys Not Selling Anything

The Mind of an American Revolutionary – Founding Father Robert Morris

The Gilded Chateau – Playing Bridge with the Nazis in Switzerland During World War II

The Idea Which Thinks Itself – Intrigue in the Great Central Valley of California

Website: www.jonfoyt.com
Email: jonfoyt@mac.com

Made in the USA
Columbia, SC
09 June 2023